A WOMAN UNHINGED

A WOMAN UNHINGED

TB MARKINSON

Published by T. B. Markinson
Visit T. B. Markinson's official website at lesbianromancesbytbm.com for the latest news, book details, and other information.
Copyright © T. B. Markinson, 2021
Cover Design by: Erin Dameron-Hill
Edited by Kelly Hashway

This book is copyrighted and licensed for your personal enjoyment only. All rights reserved. No part of this publication may be reproduced, stored in a retrieval system, or transmitted in any forms or by any means without the prior permission of the copyright owner. The moral rights of the author have been asserted.

This book is a work of fiction. Names, characters, businesses, places, events, and incidents are the product of the author's imagination or are used fictitiously. Any resemblance to actual persons, living or dead, events, or locales is entirely coincidental.

LET'S KEEP IN TOUCH

One of the best parts of publishing is getting to know *you*, the reader.

My favorite method of keeping in touch is via my newsletter, where I share about my writing life, my cat (whom I lovingly call the Demon Cat since she hissed at me for the first forty-eight hours after I adopted her), upcoming new releases, promotions, and giveaways.

And, I give away two e-books to two newsletter subscribers every month. The winners will be able to choose from my backlist or an upcoming release.

I love giving back to you, which is why if you join my newsletter, I'll send you a free e-copy of *A Woman Lost*, book 1 of the A Woman Lost series, and bonus chapters you can't get anywhere else.

Also, you'll receive a free e-copy of *Tropical Heat*, a short story that lives up to the "heat" in its name.

If you want to keep in touch, sign up here: http://eepurl.com/hhBhXX

CHAPTER ONE

"Scream if you want ice cream!" Sarah pressed her palms together and looked over her shoulder at the kids in the back of the SUV. All four yelled, followed by giggles and hand clapping.

I hunched in my seat, my fingers tightening vice-like around the steering wheel as I practically bit my tongue so I didn't holler at my wife. I hate when people shout, especially in enclosed spaces. I wanted to scream exactly that at the top of my lungs, but I didn't for several reasons. One: That would have upset the children. Two: Sarah didn't take too kindly to my buzzkill ways. Three: Screaming to say one didn't like screaming seemed counterintuitive or hypocritical, possibly both. Four: I'd recently been put on notice for not being a team player when it came to the needs of our growing family.

Sarah nudged my shoulder with a hand, her subtle way of saying *it makes the kids happy, so deal with it*. That was her go-to. The children come first. I understood that. I even wholeheartedly supported the notion. I merely wished they could be happy and silent at the same time.

The noise issue started in my childhood. I used to hide from kids my own age because children can be so annoying they're frightening. I ended up either hanging out with adults (teachers or my nanny, never my parents, whom I'd lumped into the *scary people* category), or I locked myself up in my bedroom. If the sounds were still penetrating those walls, I'd scurry under my bed, lying on my back and covering my ears. At school, I sometimes hid in the maintenance closet. To this day, the smell of Pine-Sol and bleach makes me feel safe.

Unfortunately, at this particular moment my favorite options were unavailable to me, beds and closets being in short supply while traveling in an SUV on the highway. Also, I was the driver. As a last resort, I tried locking myself inside my head, but it was difficult to stamp out everything. Occasionally, a verse of "The Wheels on the Bus" penetrated my mental walls with the sharp insistence of an ice pick against the skull.

Finally, I tried soothing my mind by imagining myself in a secluded cabin by a lake, reading a book. Someday I'd own a place by a lake. Until then, I had my red camp chair stowed in the walk-in closet for my quiet hour, which was an absolute must or I'd be unbearable to be around. I could almost smell the smoke from the make-believe cabin's imposing stone fireplace when Sarah's voice startled me back to reality.

"At the flag. The *flag*." Sarah's eyes bulged as she waved her hand repeatedly toward the driver's side window, where a red, white, and blue flag with the word *Open* on it flapped in the breeze. "Lizzie, I said turn at the flag."

"I heard you," I insisted.

I had not heard her.

My left hand hit the turn signal at the same moment I yanked the wheel to avoid missing the turn. Fortunately, given that today's adventure had dragged us to the exact middle of nowhere, there was no other traffic on the narrow country road. I pulled into a parking spot near an empty picnic table, coasting to an exceedingly gentle stop while I pretended I had not given everyone in the vehicle whiplash. Sarah was kind enough not to point it out.

"Look! Cows!" I pointed through the windshield toward a green field as the hulking beasts ambled into view. A red barn stood in the distance, and a splashing brook divided the grassy area in two. I bounced like a kid in a candy shop, breaking my own rule about being loud. Even though Sarah hadn't busted me for the noise infraction, I offered my defense by saying, "What? I love animals."

"Mooo!" Sarah said over her shoulder to the kids. At least, I assumed it was directed at them and that my sudden turn into the parking lot hadn't caused damage to the speech centers in her brain.

Troy, Sarah's step dad, pulled up next to our vehicle, and Rose, Sarah's mom, waited for me to get out of the driver's seat so we could initiate Operation Petrie Family Day Out. As she slid open the back door to start the maneuvers of getting four kids, all under the age of five, safely out of the car, Sarah made more mooing noises. The kids giggled, too distracted by her silliness to do anything but cooperate with the unbuckling of seat belts and putting on of socks and shoes that had been kicked off during the drive. The whole thing was like a well-choreographed military operation, but somehow my wife made it look effortless.

When we got all the kids to the table, Sarah whipped out a notepad and pen. "Only one person can go to the window, so what flavors do you want?"

We scanned the QR code on the table with our phones, and I eyed the choices on the online menu with a sinking feeling in my chest. "What in the fu-fudge is lavender flavor?"

Sarah snickered at my inelegant save. "Pretty sure it's *not* fudge. But I already know what you want."

I stiffened, indignant. "How do you know? There are at least fifty flavors, and I've barely read through half of them."

"Chocolate with peanut butter swirls." She crossed her arms and gave me a knowing look.

All the fight whooshed out of me because she was spot-on. "Whatever." I quickly turned my complete attention to the little ones, which may or may not have been a clever strategy to avoid having to come right out and admit that Sarah knew me better than I knew myself. "How many cows do you see, kids?"

"Thousands!" Ollie squealed without letting a second pass. So far, she'd only learned to count to fifty, but whenever possible she always shot for the moon, and I wasn't sure if she knew the word *millions* yet. I was utterly convinced this trait, among others, was going to make her teen years hard on all of us.

Fred, with his head slanted, didn't commit right away, his eyes bouncing from one sleeping cow to the next. Unlike his sister, he was interested in being correct instead of first.

Demi, our adopted daughter who was roughly half a year younger than the twins, pointed from one cow to the next, her face crinkling with the force of concentration, finally giving her answer, "Lots."

"I think you're in the right ballpark, Dem. It's more than twenty from what I can see, but well under a thousand." Ollie's focus was on something else, and I didn't think she heard me correct her guess. A good thing because she could get annoyed quickly, but we were encouraging Demi as much as possible to speak her mind. It was always a delicate line to straddle when dealing with four very different personalities who all needed careful nurturing. I started ticking off the beasts in the muddy field. I had to start over twice because a head would pop up behind another cow before settling back down out of sight. It was like they were playing a bovine version of whack-a-mole. Eventually, I gave up. "Yep. Lots."

With everyone's order jotted down in her notebook, Sarah affixed her face mask and approached one of the windows that lined half of the squat building where the ice cream was sold. The other half was some sort of farmers market, but the lights were off, and it appeared to be closed. Which made sense, given that it was only the end of March. Despite the warm weather that day, the ground was probably still too cold for planting seeds, let alone harvesting anything.

"How did Sarah hear of this place?" Rose wore a contented look as her eyes swept the rolling green pasture where the cows grazed.

"There was a post about it on the local mommy Facebook group she joined." I pointed at one of the baby cows. "Look at that one. It's black with a white stripe. It looks a little like a panda."

Rose nodded but didn't seem to be listening too closely as she scanned the massive parking lot. There were picnic tables spread out along both sides, with plenty of space to allow for social distancing without wearing masks. The relief that came from enjoying a frozen treat without fear of death still struck me as odd. The pandemic had been dragging on for ages, with no end in sight, and everything we did still involved a mental calculation of whether or not we'd die. I was so over COVID, but the virus wasn't done with humanity.

At the moment, though, we were the only ones in the lot, aside from a couple of cars that I assumed belonged to employees since there weren't any other customers in sight. Probably because, in addition to being March, it was barely after ten in the morning. Kinda early for ice cream, but that was Sarah's motive for arriving at this time. With our crew, it was best not to have a crowd, and her mom, being the oldest in our bunch, was extra cautious.

"Where?" Fred asked. This struck me as completely out of the blue, and it took me a second to understand he finally had processed my comment about the striped cow and wanted to know where it was. I pointed to the creature.

"Panna," Fred said with a big smile, swapping the D in *panda* with an extra N.

I rubbed the top of his head.

Rose held Calvin, our youngest child, on her lap, and Troy hopped up to walk with Demi and Ollie around the side of the building. Ollie never sat still for long, and Demi adored Troy, following him around like a duckling. I often wondered if her attachment to Troy was due to her missing her birth father, my brother Peter, who'd gone to prison when she was a baby.

"I can't believe it's shorts weather today." As I stretched out my legs, I could almost hear Sarah's voice in my head, telling me it wasn't. That was because we'd already had this discussion before leaving the house, when she told me that a high of sixty degrees wasn't nearly warm enough for shorts. I had disagreed and won, even if I was the only one in the group dressed that way. "After all the snow, wind, and below-freezing temps, I didn't think I'd ever be able to feel the sun on my skin again."

"It's been a long winter. With the pandemic and everything…" Rose's voice drifted off like she was too tired of the topic to finish her thought.

I grunted. "At least the vaccines are finally rolling out at a decent pace."

Rose rubbed her arm where she'd gotten her second shot three days ago. "I hear it's supposed to snow again next week."

"I swear the weather is harsher in Massachusetts. Everyone here thinks the Rocky Mountain winters are brutal, but if this year was any indication, it's much worse here. Besides, we didn't live in the mountains. That's something no one from New England seems to understand. They automatically associate Colorado with fourteeners." I became increasingly animated as I warmed to my topic. "And the number of peaks fourteen thousand feet or higher varies greatly depending on who you ask. Some say there are fifty-two in Colorado, while others claim there are actually seventy-four. A lot of the debate has to deal with the categorizing of standalone peak and subpeaks, so I guess it's no surprise people on the east coast have no clue what's in Colorado when experts fight about something that should be easily quantifiable but isn't."

"Uh-huh," Rose's eyes glazed over, and she looked like she regretted not joining Troy in exploring. It wasn't the first time something like that had happened, but once again I was left wondering why other people didn't find certain things as interesting as I did.

I returned my attention to the cows, pointing out interesting ones to Fred, who was the one kid who really got me. That's not to say the others didn't like me. They did, and that was a huge relief because my track record with family hadn't been stellar for the majority of my life.

Having been promised ice cream for several minutes now, my stomach started to rumble. When I was convinced I might die from impatience, Sarah returned to set two white cups on the table with different ice cream flavors in each. She ran back to the window for the rest while I flagged down the others. It was time to eat, and I wasn't in the mood to wait.

Troy and the girls returned first. Ollie was screaming again, but lucky for us, it was out of excitement and not one of her epic meltdowns. Aside from the obvious global pandemic issue, this was another reason it was best not to risk a crowd. Subjecting others to such an auditory assault was cruel and unusual punishment. Not that I needed a reason to avoid crowds. When it came right down to it, I didn't like people. On an individual level, there were a handful I could tolerate, but the human race as a whole? With each passing day I became more firmly convinced that human beings were terrible and deserved extinction to save the planet.

Yes, I was aware that as a mother of four I could never ever say this out loud. Not unless I wanted my ass dragged to a therapist so I could spend endless hours getting to the root of why I wanted my children to die. Because that was exactly how Sarah would choose to interpret my perfectly valid theory, while totally missing the whole *people are destroying the planet* aspect. But as long as I kept my mouth shut, I could still think it.

"Am I sharing with Freddie?" I asked, reaching for two plastic spoons.

"Yep," Sarah confirmed. "I got Ollie. Mom has Cal, and Troy is paired with Demi."

I gave Fred a spoon, but instead of carving out a massive bite the way his twin sister was already doing, he was content to draw a squiggle in the chocolate ice cream, kicking his legs without a care in the world.

"Do you want a bite?" I asked him, wondering if the frozen peanut-butter swirls were too hard for him to manage.

He nodded enthusiastically but continued creating pathways up the frozen mountain without making additional moves to act on this desire. I let him be. Fred basically had one speed, methodical.

I licked peanut butter off my spoon, bobbing my head with delight. The rich cocoa-colored ice cream, which was packed full of nutty tan rivers, was thick and gooey, not at all like ice cream that came from a supermarket. "Do you recall the first time we gave the twins ice cream?"

Sarah seemed to contemplate my question but was clearly drawing a blank. To be fair, she was more than a little distracted, struggling to keep her ice cream from falling off the table as Ollie enthusiastically removed heaping spoonfuls like she'd never see ice cream, or food, ever.

"It was after a bike ride. Remember?" I prompted. "We stopped at a place along the creek."

"That's right! What a nice memory." She gave me her *I adore you* smile, which encouraged me to continue.

"If I'm not mistaken, it was a beautiful summer day." I stared up into the sky, which was a soft blue but nothing close to the one in my memory. I blinked several times, even though the sun was behind me. "One thing I really miss is the deep blue of Colorado skies."

"Nothing can compare," Sarah agreed.

"Soon after the ice cream, Ollie had a blockbuster of a meltdown, and we had to call your mom to rescue us, but you ended up riding your bike home alone because you didn't know how to handle Troy yet since he was so much younger than your mom, and you were worried about him being a perv or something. You were wearing those red leather hiking boots you liked so much." I was feeling pretty pleased with myself, impressed by my ability to recall all the little details of such a great day. However, as my gaze wandered to Troy, I noticed his previously cheerful eyes were clouded with confusion.

That was the first clue I'd gone one teensy-tiny step too far, one of my curses.

Then I caught sight of the daggers shooting from Rose's eyes as she angrily stabbed her spoon into the ice cream, and that confirmed it. I figured she was taking her anger out on the frozen substance because we all made it a rule not to fight in front of the children.

With mounting apprehension, I swiveled my head to Sarah, dismayed at the hurt, mixed with a healthy dose of anger, in her dark brown eyes.

So much for a successful Petrie day out because I'd somehow ruined it, and it always amazed me how quickly Sarah's loving smile could turn murderous.

CHAPTER TWO

"Was it too far or too soon?" I asked. The sad part was, I really needed to know. I could tell by the reactions of everyone around me that what I had said was wrong, but as usual, I struggled to know exactly where I'd stepped off the normal path of human interactions.

"Both." Sarah's lips formed a thin line as she shook her head. "I don't understand why you don't realize that before you say things."

"I'm a slow learner." I tossed my hands helplessly in the air. "I've been trying to run things through my head first, but sometimes I get caught up in showing off, like recalling all the moments from a certain day. It's—" I ended up blowing a raspberry in frustration.

Ollie mimicked me, coupling it with, "I want ice cream!" which resulted in getting Sarah's attention off of me. Unlike most times, I was so relieved by my daughter's exuberant outburst that I gave her an encouraging smile.

Rose snorted, still not in the forgiving mood, but Troy chuckled. He never held my idiocy against me, which made him just about the only adult in the family who didn't. Sarah understood me, mostly, but there were times I knew I was too much for her.

Rose tried giving Calvin some of her vanilla ice cream with chocolate-mint chunks, but he pulled his face away, tightly scrunching his lips.

"How can a child of mine not like ice cream?" Sarah asked, seeming to let my comment slide, for the moment, but if I knew my wife, this wasn't the last I would hear of the *too far and too soon* fiasco.

"Maybe he doesn't like mint," I suggested.

Sarah offered him some of her strawberry flavor, with real berry chunks, but he balked yet again.

Troy attempted to feed Calvin a cookie dough bite, with the same resistance.

By the time Fred finally took a bite of our melting chocolate and peanut-butter treat, his sister Ollie's chin positively dripped with pink goo.

Sarah and I locked eyes, sharing amused smiles. The twins were about as opposite as could be on every front, but they were super close regardless. We didn't have to worry too much about them squabbling, aside from the types of minor scrapes that every parenting book claimed were normal. I kept an ever-vigilant eye on their interactions anyway. Given my own history with my eldest brother, I knew how quickly things could go downhill.

With their bellies full of ice cream, the kids' patience started to wear thin. Troy, who was having a hard time sitting still these days, got to his feet. Soon enough, Rose, Troy, and all the kids were exploring the accessible grounds of the farm, helping themselves to broken sugar cones in a big basket that had been set out to feed to the goats in a pen behind the building. At least that was what Sarah said the broken pieces were for.

With Sarah beside me, I continued eating my ice cream,

watching the cows. "Oh, that one is…" I squinted, not at all sure what I was seeing. "It's doing something… weird."

I watched the cow, who was laying on its stomach, rocking back and forth. After roughly thirty seconds, the cow slowly lurched to its feet. I gave the poor thing a sympathetic smile. "If it took me that much effort to get out of bed, I don't think I'd leave mine ever again."

Sarah nodded in agreement. She didn't seem to be nearly as enthralled with the cow as I was. Such interesting creatures. So large and…

"Oh. My. God." My stomach lurched, and I turned away but couldn't resist peeking through the cracks of my fingers. "Is it pooping? Please tell me it's not pooping."

"I'm pretty sure she is, indeed, pooping." Sarah didn't seem as upset as me about the defecation.

I shuddered, even as I continued to watch. "How do you know it's a she?"

"This is a dairy farm," she replied, like that was supposed to mean something to me.

I leaned forward, trying to spy the goods, or lack of them, underneath the cow, but I couldn't see a darn thing. My wife had to have superhuman vision. "Okay, I give up. How can you tell?"

"Because you only get milk from girl cows." Sarah bit down on her bottom lip, giving me an extra second to put it together in my head.

In actual fact, it took approximately four seconds for it to click. I took another long look at the beasts, my head swirling with this new revelation. "You mean all of them are girls?"

"Pretty sure." Sarah made a choking noise that was probably the sound of her swallowing a loud guffaw that was aimed squarely at me. It wouldn't have been the first time. "I doubt they'd keep any boys with the herd, except the babies. Bulls tend to cause all sorts of problems, so they have to be kept by themselves."

"Like human men," I commented, warming to the topic. "Do you think we could start keeping some of them by themselves, too?"

Sarah laughed. "We might be better off for it."

"How do you know all this stuff?" I asked, mystified.

Sarah hefted a shoulder but placed a large bite of ice cream into her mouth without saying anything more. Apparently, knowing these kinds of things wasn't as impressive to her as it was to me, and she hadn't given this particular talent much thought.

Another cow did the stomach rubbing routine, slowly getting up. My bones ached just to watch, and then the unimaginable commenced. The cow who had taken a shit right in front of me was now moving toward the small stream that divided the pasture in half. When all four legs were in the water, it stood still. A moment later, a torrent of liquid streamed from the cow's nether regions, landing with a splash.

I pointed as I screeched something unintelligible. When Sarah shot me a *what the fuck was that* look, I tried to put my horror into recognizable words. "It's peeing in the water!"

Instead of reacting with revulsion, Sarah simply bobbed her head, swishing strands of her dark pandemic hairdo, which was now well past her chin.

I repeated myself, slower this time, in case she hadn't caught on. "Urine. In. The. Water."

"Have you ever looked in a toilet?" Sarah replied dryly. "I hate to break it to you, but we pee in water, too."

"Not the water we drink." Surely that should've been obvious.

Before my shock had a chance to dissipate, more of the cows woke from their late morning nap, struggling to their feet. One by one, they lifted their tails and let loose. Poop, pee, you name it. It was going everywhere, and none of the cows seemed to care. I gagged, glancing down at my chocolate ice cream with peanut butter swirls and not liking the inevitable comparison my brain was making. "Will every single one of them have to take a shit?"

"I think that's what they do." Sarah's lips twitched. She was definitely finding amusement at my expense.

"Do they have to do it right now? I'm eating."

"I don't think they care if it bothers you," she answered with that practicality that could drive me up a wall. "This is their home. We're the invaders."

I was about to say something, but then another one started pissing, and the cow right behind her stuck its tongue out and started to drink it. I blinked three times in rapid succession, but the graphic image was still before my eyes. "That isn't happening, is it?"

Sarah, with her lips pursed, made a gagging sound. Finally, this horror show had become too much for her. It had certainly taken long enough.

"What the fu-fudge? The water is right there." I pointed to the creek where five cows now stood. "Why would they drink piss? That is messed up."

Right then, one of them pooped in the water.

"Ew!" I cringed on the wooden bench. At this point, I was fairly certain I would rather die of thirst. "Do they have mad cow disease? Is that what's going on here?"

"I don't think so." Sarah tapped the screen on her phone. "Give me a sec. There has to be a reason for the urine drinking."

I tensed as a calf approached a larger cow, fearful of what new disgusting thing might happen, but this one simply grabbed a teat and latched on. A baby cow drinking milk from a lactating mother felt much more acceptable, aside from the fact there were steaming piles of poo all around. Not to mention they were all standing in two inches of mud resulting from the recent snow melt. Clearly, cows and I do not share cleanliness standards.

The final cow stood, and I started to count in my head. When I reached ten, sure enough it was pooping. If this experience didn't scar me for life, I would be shocked.

"It's something lactating cows do." Sarah set down her phone.

"What? Feed their kids?" I gestured to the little one standing under its mom. "At least, I assume that's its mom. Then again, cows are weird. Maybe they don't care whose calf they feed."

"I was talking about drinking urine."

"That is a sentence I could have lived the rest of my life without hearing you say."

"I'll admit if someone had bet me a hundred bucks yesterday that I would say that, I would've lost."

I took a moment to stare at the incomprehensible creatures in front of us. "Are you saying this is really a thing that happens on farms?"

"We witnessed it." Sarah waved her hand to all of the evidence.

"I know, but I assumed that particular cow has issues." I circled a finger near my temple. "Honestly, I still think this herd has psychological problems."

"It says here they crave certain nutrients, and that's why they do it."

Once again, my eyes fell to my ice cream. "So, what you're saying is, I'm eating ice cream that contains milk from these cows. Not only do they live in mud and shit, but they also drink each other's urine."

"Apparently." Sarah licked her spoon clean after another lustful bite.

I pushed my ice cream cup away. "You've ruined ice cream

for me forever. Calvin is the only smart one in this family."

"How did I ruin ice cream? I'm not out there." She pointed to the cows with her spoon before dishing out another bite.

"It wasn't until you dragged me out to a farm that I learned any of this. I was perfectly content buying ice cream in the freezer aisle of a grocery store, but no. You wanted to show the kids where their food comes from. Now, I can't unsee things." I ran my palm up and down in front of my face. "This is all your fault."

"Says the woman who tossed me under the bus earlier by announcing I thought my future stepfather was a pedophile."

I groaned. I knew we hadn't finished with that conversation yet. "I didn't mean for it to come out that way because hearing you say it—" I finished the statement with a not-so-exaggerated cringe.

Her face softened. "I know you well enough to understand that wasn't your intention, but I'm also baffled as to how you thought it would be interpreted."

"I was keyed up about remembering the details about the first time the twins had ice cream."

"Lizzie—"

"It's never good when you start with my name in that tone."

She smiled. "You don't have to try so hard to impress me, Mom, or Troy. We all like you."

"It's what I do, though. Since I was a kid. It was the only way I could get attention." Also, I wasn't buying that Rose liked me. She hadn't been particularly enthused about my peak/sub-peak data points from earlier.

"I know, honey. And, I get that you're a historian. That doesn't mean you need to regurgitate our history. Especially not the bad stuff. Most definitely not with an audience. Stop thinking we're anything like your mom. We don't expect you to be dazzling every second of the day."

"Okay, but can you do one thing for me?" I swallowed,

feeling queasy. "Can you please not say regurgitate when I'm trying to block out the piss and poop machines in the field so I can attempt to enjoy the rest of my ice cream? I'd hate to throw it away. There's too much waste in this world. I don't want to contribute."

She leaned against my shoulder and kissed my cheek. "You're being very brave."

A cow mooed, and I flinched.

Sarah didn't start laughing until I did, which was another reason why I worshipped the woman. That didn't mean I stopped blaming her for teaching me about the hard truth of where my ice cream comes from because that would never happen. I could have lived my whole life not knowing about cows drinking other cows' urine like they were all members of some sort of bovine kink club.

"I'm never going to eat yellow ice cream again," I declared. Feeling relatively safe in this assertion since I couldn't think of any flavors that were that color. Rum raisin? No thank you.

Sarah quirked an eyebrow. "Brown is okay, though?"

"It's my favorite." I avoided her eyes after I said it, knowing it was a pathetic attempt to justify my idiosyncrasies.

"I do love how your brain works when it comes down to what you can and can't live without."

"Careful, I might make another decision on what, or *who*, I can live without."

"Please." This was accompanied by an impressive *eyeroll, shoulder shrug* combo that would've been the envy of many. "You wouldn't survive a day without me."

"You're right about that." I flourished my spoon in her face, and she parried with her own spoon, causing both of us to laugh. "I wouldn't, so please don't die."

"I don't plan on it, but now that you've had some ice cream, are you ready to return to a conversation topic you hate?"

"Does it involve cows drinking urine?"

"It does not." Sarah took a deep breath, which immediately put me on edge. "It involves school for the twins this fall."

"Nope." I shook my head vigorously, briefly considering raising my hands to my ears for full effect. "I'm not ready for that. We don't know what the next school year will be like. If it'll be safe. I can't send off our babies—"

"They'll be five in August. They've already missed a year of pre-K." She heaved a sigh that was bursting with frustration. "They can't miss kindergarten, too. They need to be around other kids."

"We have four children," I argued, desperation making my throat constrict so that I almost couldn't get the words out. "You make it sound like they're being raised in a Tibetan monastery."

"We can't keep our family isolated from the rest of the world. They need to go." Sarah blinked rapidly, and I was pretty sure she was trying to hold back tears. "Not to mention I need a break."

"Oh, so now our children are too much for you?" Okay, even before I said this, I knew it was way too far over that line, but I couldn't stop myself. There was a deadly disease out there I couldn't control, and people could die.

Sure enough, anger flashed in Sarah's eyes, intensified by the unshed tears. "You're not the one who's home with the kids full-time."

"I've been working from home for the past twelve months."

"Yes. You've been working. I've been taking care of the kids." Sarah balled her fists and made a grunting sound that told me she was trying to get her temper under control. I was seconds away from being in big trouble if I didn't pay close attention. "I don't think you understand. Sending the kids to school means they are not at home. For hours. It's like receiving a gift from God. You don't turn down a gift from God, Lizzie."

"I'm an atheist."

She pressed her lips together so hard they disappeared. "I know how you feel about private school, but the public schools in town are really good and—"

"No."

"You're not—"

"No." I held up my hand to show I meant business. "I want what's best for the kids, and private schools are the best."

Sarah looked like she wanted to argue, but after taking a deep breath, she said, "Fine. I've narrowed it down to two choices if we go private. I'm warning you right now, one is astronomically expensive."

"Unlike you, I don't want to deny my kids anything." Even I knew this wasn't a smart thing to say. That didn't stop me.

Instead of biting my head off, Sarah gave me a long, steady look through partially closed lids. "Cool. So, you're willing to pay twenty-five thousand?"

The best way to describe how I received this news is that it felt like someone whacked me across the chest with a two-by-four. "It costs twenty-five thousand to put two kids through six years of elementary school?"

"No. It costs that much for kindergarten. The tuition increases each year, and is over fifty grand by the time they hit middle school."

My heartrate was rapidly increasing, and my palms had started to sweat. "We're talking about the price for both the kids?"

"Each," Sarah chirped. There wasn't a doubt in my mind she was enjoying watching me suffer.

I sat up straighter on the bench, the blood pounding through my head so fast my ears were ringing. "Are you telling me that this school will charge us one hundred grand for the kids when they're eleven years old?"

"Yes."

"That's… insane." I could barely speak above a whisper, wondering if it was possible to have a heart attack on the spot. "That's the equivalent of college tuition to learn state capitals and long division. Is the other school that much?"

"Not as bad, but it's still not free."

"How much not free?" I croaked, not even caring that the sentence I'd uttered was a grammatical nightmare.

"Ten thousand each for a half day," Sarah said quietly. "Which is all we really need, since we're not looking for a childcare solution during the work day."

I ran a hand through my hair and tried to steady my breathing, but I still said, "I think I'm going into cardiac arrest."

"Pretty sure you're not."

"Won't you feel silly when I die on the spot?"

"Yes," Sarah muttered. "That's the only feeling I'd experience."

I stared at the panda-looking calf, letting out a huff of air. "I hear the public schools in town are good."

"Yes. Very."

As I was busy pouting while stewing in my own juices, the kids rounded the corner with Rose and Troy, every single one with beaming smiles. I grunted, crossing my arms. "Can I think about this?"

"Yes, but not for long. In normal times, they'd already have received their acceptance letters."

"Acceptance letters?" I let out a weak laugh. "They're going to kindergarten, not college."

Sarah placed a finger to her lips, letting me know the conversation was done for now. She turned on a thousand-watt smile for the children. "Did you guys have fun?"

"Goats!" Ollie shouted.

Freddie and Cal mimicked the sound of a goat, and Demi burst into giggles.

"Show me, please." I took Freddie and Demi's hands, while

Ollie led the way, bleating like a goat. Troy had Calvin on his hip, the boy's preferred way of moving from point A to B. All things considered, I was more than grateful for the distraction.

CHAPTER THREE

After taking the kids to a nearby park to work out the ice cream sugar high, we returned home. When I entered the kitchen with Calvin on my hip, Maddie and Willow were standing at the island, chatting. Maddie had moved with us from Colorado, and Willow moved in shortly after the declaration of the pandemic because she and Maddie had recently started dating, and neither wanted to be apart for weeks, if not months. Shortly after that, Willow lost her teaching position, making it impossible for her to continue paying rent for the apartment she wasn't even living in. Little did any of us know that a year later, Willow would still be one of the roommies in the Petrie household.

"How was the grand Petrie family adventure?" Willow dipped a shortbread cookie into a cup of tea. Judging by the completely normal color and lack of floating leaves, it wasn't one of the overly pretentious types she loved so much but might actually have been a simple cup of Earl Grey. Progress!

"The park portion of the day was fun, no trauma whatsoever." I put Calvin in his bouncy chair, placing a kiss on the top of his dark head. "The same can't be said about the ice cream. That was absolutely terrible."

"Oh no!" Willow exclaimed. "I thought the place had a ton of good reviews. The taste didn't live up to the hype?"

"The taste wasn't the issue," I said.

"Apparently, I've personally ruined ice cream forever for her," Sarah said as she entered the kitchen, holding Demi and Fred by their hands. Ollie had already zipped by to be the first to reach the art table to color.

"Yuck." I shivered at the memory, but if I was being entirely honest, the school conversation had been significantly more traumatic than learning about the strange bathroom habits of bovines. I knew my wife well enough to know this hadn't been our last conversation on the topic. Sometimes I wondered why I mounted a defense because Sarah was a force to be reckoned with. Stubbornness and idiocy were two of my strongest traits, though.

"Do I even want to know?" Maddie arched one blonde eyebrow as she shifted her gaze between Sarah and me.

"Probably not. No reason for Sarah to ruin it for everyone else in the household." I made a motion with my hand indicating this would never be talked about again, and then I scooped Gandhi into my arms, giving the terrier a kiss on the head before he conned me into an extra rawhide.

Maddie mouthed, *Later*, to Sarah, who eagerly nodded.

I did my best to pretend I didn't witness the transaction.

Willow bounced on the balls of her feet with such vigor that I had to wonder if she'd never had caffeine before. Well, aside from chocolate, but I wasn't sure that even contained enough to give anyone a buzz. If that really was Earl Grey in her mug, it seemed to be the high-octane variety. If she kept it up, I was either going to develop motion sickness or go stark raving mad.

"Where are Troy and Rose?" she asked.

"Back at their place." Sarah opened the freezer and pulled out a lasagna she'd cooked weeks ago for the days where it was easier to toss something in the oven than to make a meal from scratch.

"Right. I forgot they don't live here anymore now that she's been vaccinated." Willow glanced down at her slippered feet, perhaps having finally become as aware of the Tigger impersonation she'd been doing as I was. Her bouncing slowed considerably but didn't stop. Even so, it was an improvement.

"We're in their bubble, so we can still meet up, but I think they wanted their own space." Sarah placed a loaf of bread on the cutting board, slicing it down the middle. That meant we were having garlic bread with dinner.

The only thing was, it was kinda early in the day to be prepping the evening meal, which led me to wonder what other reason my wife might have for arming herself with a knife. Maybe she was planning to bring up the school debate again or wasn't really over the pedophile comment. Maybe she simply wanted something sharp in her hand in case I said something wrong. Which, given enough time, I certainly would.

A vivid picture formed in my mind of Sarah telling a police officer, "I don't know how it ended up in her heart. One second, I was cooking dinner, and the next, Lizzie was dead on the kitchen tile. Would you like some garlic bread? It's fresh out of the oven."

She'd probably get away with it, too. Her garlic bread was delicious.

"Lizzie, you got a minute?" Willow was practically doing jumping jacks now, and I was starting to understand why she avoided caffeine and stuck to her snobby herbal brands. Had she switched due to the price? Perhaps the more important question was would she ever be able to stand still again? The thought of having inadvertently turned the woman into a perpetual motion machine killed any giddiness I'd felt over converting her to normal tea.

"Yep. My offi—the library?" Dammit. I'd caught myself, but not before the flash of disapproval in Sarah's eyes that was visible from all the way across the room.

With as many people as we had living under our roof, Sarah had grown tired of my desire to divide up the house into Lizzie spaces and what the rest of them could have. Apparently, that wasn't how she saw things. For weeks now, I'd been trying to stop referring to the library as my office, even though it was, in fact, my office and my Zoom classroom.

The instant Willow nodded, Maddie led the remaining kids to the front room. From the precision of the maneuver, I was immediately certain I'd been ambushed. It was never good. I was especially nervous because I didn't have any of the children with me for protection, by which I mean that if I didn't like what was being said, I could always get out of it by exclaiming, "Oh, no! Ollie has her head stuck in a plastic container again."

Hang on. Did that scenario imply I had slipped the item in question over Ollie's head to help make my escape? Also, Willow would witness me doing that. Strike that. I'd feign something that didn't put any of the children in harm's way. Sudden onset lactose intolerance, maybe. After all, my tummy was a little grumbly after that rich ice cream.

Willow motioned for me to head to the library, but I stalled long enough to grab a cold water from the fridge. My eyes landed on a container of milk, reinforcing my emergency plan. Yes, lactose intolerance was the thing to keep in my back pocket, just in case.

We settled on the couches in the library, and I guzzled water from my metal thermos before asking, "What's up?"

"Have you heard of Anne Geary?" Willow asked, which I'll admit had not been anywhere on my list of reasons to be ambushed.

Relaxing a little, I tried to think whether I knew the person Willow had mentioned, and why I should. Nothing came to me. I tilted my head toward the ceiling as if a clue to the mystery woman's identity would be there. It wasn't, but I hate to admit flat-out not knowing something, so I replied cautiously, "The name rings a bell, but I can't quite place it at the moment."

"She teaches at Yale," Willow prompted.

I snapped my fingers, suddenly able to picture the woman's face in my head. "That's right. I met her at a conference a few years ago. She seemed nice. Why are you asking?"

"You haven't signed up for her newsletter?"

I frowned, still perplexed by where this conversation was going. "Not that I know of. Why?"

"Let me show you." Willow pulled out her phone, tapped the screen a few times, and then handed it to me.

I skimmed the page in question, quickly surmising that it was an article about the Civil War era, which made sense as I now recalled that was Professor Geary's specialty. "This is interesting. I never made this connection with the history of Maine and the abolition movement in the 1800s. American history baffles me sometimes. So much racism."

"Says the expert on Nazis." Willow bounced on the sofa cushion, bubbling with either excitement or tea. I wasn't sure which. "I think you and I should start a newsletter and podcast like Anne Geary's."

"But… I know nothing about Maine. I haven't even been there since we moved here with the kids." I stroked my chin, deep in thought. "No, we did drive through once, but I don't think we can go there yet. Not with the COVID restrictions. Also, my Civil War background is minimal at best. I wonder if Sarah would help me plan a Civil War battleground family road trip. Is that too macabre for kids?"

"Uh, Lizzie," Willow began, but I was already on a roll,

loving the way ideas formed in my head, not stopping. Honestly, it was always such a rush.

"It might be better if I don't tell them that the limbs they sawed off after the Battle of Antietam could be stacked a mile high. Hey, I guess I do remember some things from my undergrad days!" I tapped my finger against my chin. "How do they know that, really? Did someone actually stack all the bloody stumps and measure them? That'd take a really tall ladder, but that doesn't make sense. A ladder a mile high?" My brow furrowed, trying to imagine this.

Willow gaped at me but then made beeping sounds like a truck backing up. "Don't go too far down the wrong path."

My whirling brain screeched to a halt as it struck me I'd misinterpreted something. I took a stab at identifying the error. "You didn't mean you wanted us to start a Civil War newsletter with a Maine connection?"

"Why on earth would I want that?" Willow's facial muscles twitched, and she looked like she was somewhere in that gray area between laughing and crying, which is an expression I'm pretty familiar with seeing on other people's faces. "We can't compete with Geary on that front, anyway, and I'm not sure the world really needs two such newsletters."

"Then, what are you suggesting?" I asked, deciding it was safer not to take a second guess.

"Given the rapid increase of the wealth gap, coupled with the rise of white supremacy, it got me thinking. If we blended what we both know…" She paused and then clarified, possibly because of my rambling about Maine and the Civil War, "My studies of the Gilded Age and yours on the Nazis, we can offer insight into the troubling trends today that are eerily familiar."

"That could be a fun project." I perked up considerably at this prospect, vaguely aware that my definition of fun was different from most. That didn't matter now. I only needed to convince one person it was a good idea. How would I pose it to

Sarah? Unfortunately, she knew when I got involved with a project, I dove in headfirst.

Also, I needed to see if she would consider the battlefield road trip. Now that the idea had penetrated my brain, I really liked it. Maybe we should start with the Revolutionary War, considering we were living in Massachusetts. Who knew when we could leave the state safely? Would a PowerPoint presentation help my cause with Sarah? I could use the children as my excuse, like she did when doing things I didn't like, such as screaming in enclosed spaces.

Could this be an argument for homeschooling the kids? I was about to get up from the sofa and fire up my laptop to start drafting some slides when Willow snapped her fingers to recapture my attention.

"Not just fun, Lizzie, but lucrative. Anne is pulling in a million a year."

"What?" I nearly dropped Willow's phone, and to avoid disaster in case there was another bombshell in store, I handed it back to her. "How much are you paying for that newsletter?"

"It's free," Willow explained, "but for those who like a deeper dive, there's an option to pay for premium content. Then there's her podcast, which is one of the top three overall, not only among history podcasts but across the board. It garners millions of listens a month, which means she has sponsors and advertising."

"You want to do a podcast with me?" I wasn't an obvious choice for a few reasons. For instance, I still couldn't puzzle out the limb-stacking trivia. However, a million dollars was a big incentive, and extra money would make raising four kids in an expensive place like the northeast a whole lot easier to swallow. To be sure she wasn't pulling a prank, I glanced around the room to see if anyone was lurking in the shadows to pop out and yell, "Psych!" But no one did, so I asked, "Why me?"

Willow laughed in her carefree way. "Because we'd make a

great team. You have experience in broadcasting now with JJ's show."

"You're on it, too." True, I had experience, but it was always difficult for me to grasp why people trusted my abilities. If they spent a day in my head, they'd understand how inept I really am. It was only a matter of time until my house of cards crashed down around me, resulting with everyone pointing and yelling, "She's a fraud!"

"I'm still a newbie, though. It'd be good to have a pro to steady the ship." She held a hand out, steady as a rock, which only proved she didn't need me. Besides, my hands always shook a little, a side-effect of my Graves' disease.

As for the podcast, I couldn't help but be suspicious. Was this Sarah or Maddie's idea, and they were forcing Willow into asking me? I tossed Sarah out of the hat right away because she was already frustrated with me for not doing enough around the house. No way would she want to keep me even busier so she'd have to take on more work. Maddie, though, had motive. When Willow had first moved in, I wasn't a happy camper. Did Maddie think if Willow bit the bullet and gave me a reason to keep her around, I wouldn't want either of them to ever move out?

I had to stop myself because once my brain got going down the garden path of conspiracy theories, it'd take monumental efforts to get me back to reality.

"I don't know," I finally said, which was about as true a statement as there ever was. The whole thing had caught me completely by surprise, and I had no frame of reference for how to feel about it. Other than the fact my first impulse is always to say no. In that respect, Willow was lucky she was catching me in an inquisitive mood.

"Think about it," Willow urged, her eyes on mine. "We can tap into JJ's *Matthews Daily Dish* audience, and I'm confident other history and news nerds will follow. A lot of people are concerned about things these days. I really think we should get going on this. I've outlined five topics to get us started."

She handed me her phone again, but this time it was open to a sheet in her Notes App. She'd neatly outlined key issues, complete with five bullet points for each. It was a sharp presentation, come to think of it. Maybe PowerPoint was passé, and I should consider using a format like this to present my homeschooling argument to Sarah.

Willow cleared her throat, holding her hand out for the phone. I returned it as I scooted my attention back to the matter at hand, which, as I saw it, had one major roadblock to overcome.

"How do I get Sarah to green-light this?" I looked expectantly at Willow, hopeful that she'd anticipated this issue and might already have a suggestion or two. Because taking on more work wouldn't win me any team-player points on the home front, but on the other hand, it would add a tick in the good provider column. Maybe that would be enough.

"You like the idea?" Willow was bouncing again. It seemed to be purely from excitement now, but on the off chance it wasn't, I made a mental note to add decaffeinated tea to the shopping list.

"I love it," I admitted, surprising myself. I started to envision all the books and documentaries I wanted to explore, which would lead down so many wondrous rabbit holes. Maybe I should set up a desk in the walk-in closet to accompany my red chair. I could lose myself for hours and hours.

And hours…

"Tell her that," Willow suggested, dragging my brain away from its closet happy place, at least temporarily. "She adores you, so I'm sure she'll be thrilled to know you've found something you're excited about. But don't forget to mention the million bucks possibility, too."

"Smart thinking," I said. "She'll worry I'm going to drown

myself in research, and we both know I will absolutely do that. But for a million dollars, she might be willing to let it slide."

My brain was already racing back to the comfort of my red camp chair. What color pen should I dedicate to this research project? Red? No, too much like blood, given the topic. Green? Nope. Too hard to read. Purple? If I could find a dark violet, that would be perfect. Different, but cheerful enough to avoid the darkness that plagued me, and this project wasn't going to offer a lot of chuckles.

"I know how Sarah and Maddie—mostly Maddie—give you a lot of shit," Willow said, a sympathetic expression on her face, "but when push comes to shove, they admire your dedication."

"How do you know that's what Maddie thinks?" I sucked in my lips, unsure if I really wanted to know. "Sarah tells me she admires that about me sometimes, but your girlfriend can be kinda mean." Hence why I'd been dodging her for many months while my brain sorted through some recent revelations. There was only so much I could handle at one time, and sometimes it was hard to pinpoint which I'd been avoiding the most: COVID or Maddie.

"Trust me. Maddie thinks the world of you, but she doesn't know how to show it. I think it stems from her feeling inadequate. Her dad is a bigwig in finance. Then she was engaged to Peter and had to compete with all the Petries."

"Peter isn't much competition these days," I said, unable to completely hold back a chuckle over my sibling's self-inflicted misfortune. "He's out of prison, but he can't leave the house, or his ankle thingy will go off, and no employer will touch him with a ten-foot pole."

"Yeah, I don't know why Maddie would be competitive when you're so chill about things." Willow laughed good-naturedly as she added, "This is a tough circle to run in."

With Peter out of a job and my father's forced retirement,

did that make me the leader of the Petrie pack? My heart experienced a little thrill until I remembered the other thing. The autism thing, or the *A-secret,* as I'd come to think of it. Would I be able to rise above it, or would that continue to keep me at the bottom of the Petrie ladder, like a boot on my throat?

CHAPTER FOUR

A FEW DAYS after my chat with Willow about the new project, I finished reading one of the books she'd suggested. There was no way to put this, except to say I was hooked and wanted to go full-steam ahead. Which meant I needed to broach the subject with Sarah. Taking in a fortifying breath, I pushed myself away from my desk to search her out.

I found Sarah at the kitchen table with Freddie, Ollie, and Demi. They were decorating Easter sugar cookies, even though the holiday was a couple weeks away.

"This looks like fun!" I took a seat, grabbing a cookie from the rack to smear cream cheese frosting on it. "Is this a rabbit?"

"Theoretically." Sarah was adding sprinkles to an egg-shaped cookie. "You're in a really good mood."

"It's almost Easter," I explained. "It's my favorite holiday."

"You're an atheist," she reminded me without pausing in her cookie decoration.

"What does that have to do with loving Easter? The weather is getting better. Ham is on the menu, not turkey." I made a gagging sound, which I followed up by saying, "Yuck" in case she didn't quite get how much I despised turkey. Dry and tasteless in my opinion.

Sarah started on a carrot-shaped cookie. "That's really the reason for your giddiness?"

No doubt about it. She wasn't taking the bait. Buying myself some time, I leaned over and checked out Freddie's cookie, noting he'd carefully placed a heart-shaped sprinkle for the bunny's nose and added blue sprinkles for whiskers. "Nice job, Fred!"

Olivia had a different concept in mind, which consisted of smothering hers with such a thick layer of sprinkles it was impossible to see a speck of the frosting. I could almost hear the crunching sound that cookie would make when she tried to bite through the hard candy shell. "Ooooh, I like the dedication, Ollie."

Ollie released an evil giggle, the kind that, despite her being my child—or perhaps because of it—made the hair stand up on the back of my neck. We were going to have our hands full with this one.

Ignoring any evidence our nearly five-year-old daughter was hatching a sinister plot, Sarah selected the bottle of green sprinkles to form the top of her carrot. "Are you going to confess about your good mood yet or continue to try to avoid my question by using our children for cover?"

Damn. She was onto me.

I looked up from smearing frosting on my cookie, which had just as overabundant a layer of frosting as Ollie's did of sprinkles. "I'm being completely honest. I really don't like Thanksgiving. As a matter of fact, why do we keep serving turkey? Most people don't like it. We should think outside of the box. Unless you're talking stuffing, which should always come from a box. Just the way it is, without all those vegetables they tell you to add."

"What, in your esteemed opinion, would make a better Thanksgiving meal?"

"Spaghetti would be way better." I held my hand above my head to illustrate how much. "Or Mac and cheese."

"You always crave simple meals."

"I'm not a fan of mixing a lot of ingredients. I find it overwhelming. Like a ham and cheese sandwich. All you need is bread, ham, and cheese. Nothing else. Don't destroy a good thing by adding condiments and veggies. They ruin everything." I punctuated this with an emphatic jab of my finger in the air.

Sarah drilled her dark eyes into my blues, and I could see at once that she was after something, though I didn't know what. I shivered as if she could yank the truth from my soul. "I do enjoy how hard you try to get me off the scent by talking about everything else under the sun but the one thing I want to know."

"We were talking about Thanksgiving," I argued, searching my brain for the source of her displeasure. "Did you want me to use a turkey and cheese sandwich as my example? No can do. I hate turkey so much I can't even use it for a hypothetical. I think you're missing the key piece of information in this conversation."

"I want to know why you're in such a good mood," Sarah prodded, her voice telling me she wanted the answer now.

"Oh, that." Honestly, I'd completely forgotten the track of the conversation. I really took sandwich making to heart. Now, I had to kick my brain back into gear and try to remember why I was so happy, aside from ham. Was it from cookie decorating with my wife and four kids? No. There were only three. "Hey! Where's Calvin?"

"Taking a nap, and you're still stalling."

"I think showing concern for our youngest is a vital ingredient for being a loving, not to mention, responsible parent." I finished with the frosting and selected pastel-colored balls to decorate it. "Besides, all this talk about food is making me hungry. Is it bad manners to eat the cookie before I finish decorating it?"

"You have five seconds to come clean before I take your cookie away."

"Why are you being a Grinch?" No, that was Christmas. "What's the Easter equivalent for that?"

"Elmer Fudd," Sarah deadpanned.

"Well, maybe. He does hunt Bugs Bunny, after all." I did my best Elmer Fudd impression, "I'm hunting wabbits."

"One…" Sarah drummed her fingers on the table, and I marveled at how her brain never went off the rails like mine did.

"I'm hunting wabbits" Olivia repeated with such a dead serious tone it made my eyes widen.

"Good job, Ollie," I told her, fighting the urge to be creeped out by the fact my kid had been possessed by the ghost of Elmer Fudd. "Maybe voice-overs are in your future. What about you, Fred? Can you say, I'm hunting wabbits?"

He cocked his head, thinking.

"Two…" Sarah tried sounding tough, but she was grinning at Ollie's impersonation.

"Demi. Your turn." I motioned for her to do her best.

"Wabbits!" She seemed about as taken aback as me. Ever since she'd moved in with us, after her mom's death and when Peter went to prison, Demi held her tongue 99.879 percent of the time.

"We have a winner!" I high-fived Demi while Sarah distracted Ollie by cooing over Ollie's monstrosity of a decorated egg cookie. This was a necessity so Ollie wouldn't get upset that I gave Demi praise.

Sarah didn't so much as pause to take a breath before she said, "Four…"

"You skipped three." I stuck out my bottom lip, but before Sarah could say five, I rushed to say, "Willow mentioned a business venture that sounds exciting, and I've spent the last few days digging into it. I have to admit, it's invigorating to test drive a new research project."

"Oh?" Sarah jerked her head back, clearly not expecting that answer from me.

"We're going to—" I quickly corrected to, "We're thinking of starting a newsletter and podcast together."

She nodded thoughtfully. "That does seem right up your alley, but is that really the reason for your good mood."

"Partly. I really do love spring. This winter has been so fudging hard."

"Fudge!" Ollie parroted, but her tone had more menace than mine. Despite that, I gave her a high five.

Fred blurted, "I'm hunting wabbits!"

"Great job, Fred!" Sarah clapped her hands.

I gave him an approving smile, and he tucked his chin down to refocus his attention on his cookie masterpiece.

"Let's get back to the food situation. I'm starving." My stomach backed me up by rumbling.

"How can you always be hungry?"

"Hey, I have a thyroid problem. Don't be—" I couldn't think of the right word because racist was wrong. I resorted to shaking my cookie at her, and it cracked in half. "Well, I guess I have to eat it now."

Sarah laughed. "You did that on purpose."

"You can't prove it." I chomped into my cookie. "So good."

Ollie didn't waste a second, chomping into the overly decorated monstrosity, and Demi took a dainty bite of hers.

"Such a great example you're setting." Sarah ate one.

"I know. It's terrible of me to have fun with my family. It's probably criminal in some parts of the world."

Sarah rolled her eyes. "Tell me more about the newsletter."

Around a bite, I managed to say, "Not much to tell yet. I wanted to run the idea by you first before getting too far into the weeds."

"Let me guess. You warned Willow that I might say no?"

"Yes… er… Did she already tell you, or did you trick me?" I put my hands on my hips. "You tricked me, didn't you?"

"You can't prove it." She stuck out her tongue, which was speckled with different pastel colors from the sprinkles.

"Nicely played." I looked to the kids. "Isn't your mom super smart?"

They nodded, but Ollie hooked her thumb toward her chest, saying, "I'm super smart."

"That you are." Using one of the piping bags with pink icing, I spelled out the word smart on a cookie, to the best of my ability. It was safe to say, cake decorator wasn't in my future. "What does this say?"

The trio chorused the answer, bringing a proud smile to my face.

"Let's do a more challenging one." I selected a cookie that was more oval in shape to give me more room to work with. "And this word?" It spelled out family, something I was always reinforcing to our children. The importance of our family sticking together.

They sounded it out, to varying degrees of success, and Sarah had to wipe away a small tear. I took that as a win and didn't press for her blessing for the new project since she'd kinda already given it without saying so explicitly. Besides, if she hated the idea, I would've known it by now because she was never shy about telling me her thoughts when it came to something she disagreed with. Me, I hated confrontation, but Sarah took it head-on. Maybe that was why we worked. The whole *opposites attract* thing. Whatever the reason, I blew her a kiss and started on a second cookie before heading back to my office—er, library to start reading the next book on my list.

CHAPTER FIVE

THE NEXT MORNING, birdsong roused me from an uneasy sleep. I rolled onto my back, tossing an arm over my eyes, not wanting to face the day yet.

Sarah rolled over and placed a hand on my chest. "It's going to be okay."

I lifted my arm enough to crack one eye open. "How did you know I was worried?"

"Aside from you tossing and turning all night long?"

I responded with a groan, covering my eyes again. "I'm sorry."

"It's fine. But I know you. Your doctor's appointment is probably one of the last things you want to do today." While her voice was thick with sleepiness, she tried to use her soothing tone. The one she saved for a kid or Lizzie meltdown.

My stomach clenched at the very mention of the word *doctor*. I wanted to pull the covers up over my head and never come out. "I wish you could go with me. Help me explain... things. I'm not good on that front."

To her credit, her face didn't blare with the agreement that observation deserved. "I wish I could, too, but with COVID, no one else is allowed in the exam room. Remember, it's only the first step. You're going for your physical, and when she asks if you have any concerns, tell her all of them."

"My allergies," I said, ticking off the top item on my mental list.

"Yes. They've been so much worse since we moved here." Sarah held up a finger. "That's one. What else?"

"My trouble sleeping."

"Yep, that's another one." She added a second finger, and I experienced a flush of pride at getting the answer correct. I like being right almost as much as I dislike doctors.

"Can you write the rest out on a piece of paper?" I begged as my brain failed to produce anything else, even though I knew those were far from my only concerns of late. "I don't have a great track record of getting doctors to listen to me. It took forever for a doctor to figure out my thyroid issue, and that was after years of me making appointments with every specialist under the sun to finally receive a correct diagnosis. I knew something was seriously wrong, but doctors don't listen. Especially to women."

"You're seeing a woman doctor," Sarah said in an encouraging tone that utterly failed to convince me.

"Doesn't matter. I saw several female doctors who disregarded my complaints back then. Now, I'm seeking clarification about something that not many understand because the vast majority don't think girls have it, and the test for it is geared for boys. How do I get help for…?" I stopped, unwilling to say the dreaded A-word out loud. "I don't have a special mark on my forehead or something, ergo, it can't be… *that*."

"Honey, we have to set the doubters aside. Fuck them. This is about you. It won't change who you are, but it might free you to know for certain whether or not you're—"

"Don't say it!" I screeched, flinching like the word itself could deal a physical blow. "And I know. It's just… I have such a hard time describing things. Words fail me. I've found doctors speak too quickly. They never listen. I don't know how to say, 'Slow down; I don't understand.'"

"Say it like that." Sarah, ever the optimist, was adamant it was that easy.

"I can with you because you know me, and you won't judge me. It's an entirely different kettle of fish with someone I don't know. My defenses go up immediately. I can't show weakness. My family always pounced when I did. My brain has learned this, so…" I let my voice trail off.

Sarah cupped my cheek. "I know. Remember, I'll be in the car in the parking lot."

"I want you in the room." I made a strangled noise that was half whimper and half groan. "I better get in the shower."

"Mom's coming over to take the kids to her house so Troy can help her watch them while we're at your appointment."

"Why does life have to keep punching me in the gut, even during a pandemic?"

By five minutes to nine, Sarah pulled into the parking lot of the doctor's office, and I froze in the passenger seat.

"Remember," Sarah said, placing a hand on my knee and giving it a supportive squeeze. "Three things. Allergies. Sleeping. And—"

My hands flew to cover my ears. "Don't say it."

"I'll be right here." She gave my knee another pat before withdrawing her hand.

"Can you go in for me?" I whined.

"I really wish I could, but I can't," she answered, ever the practical one. "Aside from addressing the three things, you need to have a primary care doctor established in case something happens. You already had to wait five months for this appointment. This isn't the time to be without a doctor."

"Grown-up Lizzie understands the reason I'm seeing this person. Not-so-grown-up Lizzie says let's go home and watch movies in bed. We can watch your favorite: *Bridges of Madison County*. Or we can go for ice cream. Even if the cows shit and piss the entire time. I won't make a peep." I mimed locking my lips and tossing the key into the back seat.

"We'll go for ice cream after your appointment and watch the movie tonight."

"Hold on," I said, shaking my head at having walked right into that trap. "I suggested the movie in lieu of the appointment. Watching it tonight defeats the purpose of me trying to bribe you."

"No take backs. Now go." She flicked her hands to get me moving, but her sexy smile gave me incentive to stay.

I stuck my tongue out at her before slipping on a face mask as I opened the car door. A red sign hung on the front door of the medical building, saying to wait there before being allowed inside. On the table by the door was an industrial size bottle of hand sanitizer. I pumped some into my hands and waited.

A minute later, a masked nurse waved me inside.

She asked me the questions that were becoming the new normal. Did I have any symptoms? Had I been in contact with someone who'd tested positive? I answered no, and she aimed a thermometer at my head, wrote the number down on a Post-it note, and slid a pulse oximeter onto one of my fingers. She jotted the reading onto the same piece of paper, but her expression gave no indication whether the number was good or bad.

When she'd finished, she ripped the page off the pad and handed it to me. "Give this to the nurse."

I was confused because I thought she *was* the nurse, but I looked around and spotted a different nurse. That one was speaking to a patient, so I quickly assessed the woman who'd handed me the slip probably didn't mean I should give it to the first nurse I saw. She must have meant the one who would lead me into the exam room. Still, for someone who hates doctor's offices and is never at her best before an exam, this could've been made clearer.

Before I could do anything, I still had to check in with the front desk. That woman gave me paperwork to fill out since this was my first visit. Why couldn't my intake forms travel to the next office to avoid filling out the same details over and over? I really wanted to ask, but I suspected it would get me into trouble, and if they had to march me back out to where Sarah was waiting in the car without having completed my appointment, I would never hear the end of it.

In the waiting room, I sat in a chair in the corner as far away as possible from everyone. Pre-COVID, this would have clued others in that I didn't like being around people, which I didn't. Now, I'd be considered abnormal if I sat right next to someone. That was one of the only good things about the pandemic. I didn't have to pretend so much and try to make small talk with people I didn't want to converse with and probably would never see again. I've always found useless human interactions draining.

After completing the work, I returned the clipboard and retook my seat, waiting to be called into the exam room. To pass the time, I read a book on J.P. Morgan. Though I had several books I needed to read to prepare a lecture for my next class, this wasn't one of them. However, since I studied the Nazis, all of my research books had swastikas on them, and I've found people give you really funny looks if you carry around books with swastikas on them in public.

Well, maybe not so much these days. Lately, it seemed like I spent a lot more time wondering if the person who was staring at me was shocked by my reading choice (which, again, I want to stress was for work) or if they were trying to figure out an angle to say, "I'm kinda into that as well. Let's talk." Not because they were a historian like me but an actual fascist wannabe, and the current political climate let them freely fly their authoritarian flag.

Did I mention how I don't like people?

After marking up two pages, because I could never read a biography without taking notes in the margins, a woman opened the door and called out my name. My instinct was to hide behind my book and not acknowledge that I was the Elizabeth Petrie she was looking for. Considering I had already filled out the paperwork, and there was only one other person in the waiting area, I reluctantly responded to avoid being called out on my childishness. I didn't want to earn a bad mark in my file.

Here goes nothing.

We walked down a bleak white corridor, took a right to another drab hallway, and then entered an exam room. She motioned for me to take a seat in the chair next to the exam table. She sat at a computer on the opposite side, with her back to me, and began the intake portion of the physical.

I confirmed my name and birth date. Then the easy part ended, and I had to step onto the scale. It was an old fashioned one with the sliding bar. I watched the nurse plunk the metal marker into the slot that corresponded with my usual weight and breathed a sigh of relief, patting myself on the back that there had been no *Pandemic Twenty* for me. But then she nudged the marker with her finger, once and then again. Still the bar refused to balance in the parallel position where it belonged.

"It's broken," I informed her helpfully.

"Nope. I need to move this top one up by ten pounds and try again." She pinched the marker with her fingers, but I slapped at her hand before she could move it. She crossed her arms and took a step backward.

"You're doing something wrong." I shifted my weight to my left foot, then to my right, scowling as the scale refused to balance no matter what I tried. Also, this was the wrong time to remember I still wore my sneakers. Luckily, I wore shorts, not pants. Would that balance out my shoe weight?

"Are you done?" The nurse gave me a withering look. I stood still while she adjusted the device, but I closed my eyes so I wouldn't have to see the damage.

After an excruciating six minutes spent dredging up every medical complaint I'd ever had in my life—which I swear she took joy in after the scale incident—we got to my thyroid issue. I had to repeat three times that I no longer took medicine for it. I was starting to wonder why this woman became a nurse. Her empathy was severely lacking, and her slumped shoulders and repeated long sighs whenever I mentioned something that involved her typing the information into my electronic file made it abundantly clear she wanted to be somewhere else.

Join the club!

Then, I reminded myself that she was working in a doctor's office in the middle of the pandemic. If I were in her shoes, would I be super thrilled to expose myself to the plague five days a week? Definitely not. Which meant I didn't have to be her best friend, but it was probably not okay to wish her dead. I can be as reasonable as the next person when the situation calls for it.

"Okay, the doctor will be with you shortly. Please change into the gown." She shut the door.

I started to remove my top, but the nurse barged in again.

"I'm not ready yet!"

She stared at me with dead eyes, uttered an oh, and stepped back out.

So far, there were two marks against this office: no empathy and total rudeness.

Once I'd slipped on the gown, which was made of thick tissue paper, I hopped onto the table. It was covered in a sheet of white paper similar to the rolls of craft paper Sarah bought the children, but given it was in a medical facility, it no doubt cost considerably more. It crinkled unpleasantly beneath me. The only thing that would have made me feel less comfortable and more ridiculous was if they'd insisted I top off the outfit with a paper party hat.

The door opened, and another woman, presumably the doctor based on her white coat, said, "Good morning, Elizabeth. How are you today?"

"Fine," I grumbled. I hated my full name, and we'd never met, so why was she acting like we were friends?

The doctor took a seat at the computer and started to interrogate me on everything I'd already supplied answers for to the nurse, which raised an important question. Why did the nurse ask if the doctor was going to go through each one in what I would classify as an excited chipmunk voice? It seemed to take forever...

"Let's take a looksee." She hopped up from the seat.

Looksee? I didn't like her word choice because I was pretty sure it wasn't actually an acceptable medical term, but whatever. At this point, I wanted to get the whole thing over with and run back to the car.

"Your skin is very dry," she informed me, squinting at my forearm with distaste. "You need to drink more water."

She shined a light into my eyes, asking me to look to the right, left, up, and down. I complied, nearly falling off the table. Finally, she looked up my nose. "Just what I thought. Your nose is dry. You need more water."

Now that we'd reached the appropriate body part, I knew Sarah would kill me if I didn't get started on the list. "Since moving here, I've been having a terrible time with my allergies."

The doctor nodded slowly. "More water will help."

"I drink a lot of water." I stared at my bag next to the chair, eyeing my water bottle in the side mesh pocket, which I'd drained once before my appointment and was halfway through it again. "Isn't there anything else?"

"You can always drink more." Her chipmunk voice was even higher, like she'd sucked on a helium balloon.

I'm not a fucking camel, bitch.

She made me hop off the table, telling me to raise my arms and resist her pressing down on them. Then she had me turn this way and that. She spoke so rapidly I had no idea what in the fuck she wanted me to do. When this part was done, she had me get back on the table for a breast exam and Pap smear.

I took this moment to mention my sleeping issues, perhaps because the thought of having either of these promised procedures would certainly lead to nightmares.

Again, she urged me to drink more water, which didn't make sense because if I drank a lot of water before bed, wouldn't I need to constantly get up to pee? Clearly, this woman was a one-solution kind of doctor.

"Anything else?" she asked as she ripped off her gloves and replaced them with a different pair.

Yeah. What do you recommend if I get thirsty?

I sat up, not wanting to say another word, but I'd promised Sarah I would. "Uh, yeah… I've been doing some research, and I think… I might have some signs of autism."

Like every single one.

I tensed as she cocked her head and gave me a long look. Since she wore a mask, I couldn't see her full expression, but her eyes seemed to twinkle with amusement. "Let's see if that's possible."

This confused me. Was she going to wave a magic wand to expose whether or not I had a certain aura or some shit like that? Instead, she went back to the computer. "You're in your thirties."

"Yes," I said, even though she hadn't stated it as a question.

"You're a professor."

"Yep." Where was she going with this?

"You're married with children."

"Yeah."

"You've made eye contact with me through most of this appointment."

This time I didn't say a word, knowing that she'd assessed in our short, non-stop episode of her barking of orders or asking questions that I didn't meet her qualifications for anything. Not allergies, nor sleep problems, and apparently not the A-word.

"Should I just drink more water, then?" I asked sarcastically, imagining shoving a hose down her throat to blast the stick out of her ass.

However, she didn't seem to pick up on my *I think you're a fucking kook* vibe and cheerily replied, "Absolutely. It's the miracle drug."

CHAPTER SIX

Hurriedly, I put my clothes back on and stormed out of the office.

Sarah, who was sitting in the driver's seat where I'd left her what felt like a decade ago, looked up from her phone and smiled at me through the windshield.

After shoving my shoulder bag onto the floor, not bothering to place it in the back seat like I usually did, I climbed into the passenger seat. I wanted to get the fuck out of Dodge.

My wife knew me better than anyone, but in case she had yet to pick up on the subtext in me shoving my bag onto the floor, I made a point of crossing my arms and giving her my harshest *I told you so* glare.

Despite all of this evidence that the appointment had gone epically wrong, she said as cheerily as possible, "How'd it go?"

I gritted my teeth. "Apparently, I should drink more water."

"Everyone should," she said with a shrug, clearly not understanding the depths of my frustration. Yet. But she soon would. "What did she say about your allergies?"

"I should drink more water."

"The problems sleeping?" Her confident tone started to flag, but I saw her push through it by keeping her smile firmly affixed.

"Water."

"The other thing?" Sarah swallowed, though it was hard to tell whether she was afraid the doctor had given the same answer or the one I'd been dreading.

"Water."

Sarah blinked hard, which I think was code for *Are you fucking serious?*

"According to the doctor—that *you* chose for me, I will remind you—a woman in her mid-thirties who has a steady job and can look people in the eye can't be placed into the A-word box."

"Did she say that exactly?"

"Exactly, no. But essentially, yes." I repeated the conversation to the best of my ability. The only thing that made it bearable was witnessing Sarah's anger rise with each word until I was fairly certain we were on the same page at last.

"Okay." Sarah stared through the windshield as if she wanted to have a word or two with the doctor. "That settles it. This woman isn't the doctor for you. Good to know. Let's go."

I slapped my forehead. "I forgot to check out with the front desk. Should I go back in?"

"Our insurance covers a yearly physical. If there are other charges, let them bill us." She started the car engine, giving the gas pedal a rev for good measure. "I'm sorry, honey. Not all doctors are good."

"I know that. I mean, given my history, I don't have a high bar, but I'm kinda shocked. This is one of the most liberal areas in Massachusetts, and all that lady could say was drink more water. Why did she even go into medicine if her goal was to ignore people and their issues? I'm sick and tired of the medical profession ignoring women simply because of our gender. It's criminal."

"Do you still want to get some ice cream?"

I shook my head, my lower lip protruding in a pout. "I want to go home and take a shower. I feel violated."

Sarah didn't say another word, steering us home.

When I finished with my shower, Sarah was in the bathroom, reading her phone.

As I toweled dry, she said, "You're right. I've been reading some of that doctor's reviews, and the people who simply needed their yearly physical done and nothing else seemed to like her. But those seeking treatment for something more complicated than a cold said she doesn't listen. When I checked out the reviews, I didn't dig deep enough. I'm so sorry to have put you through that."

"It's not your fault," I said, any desire I may have had to blame Sarah until the end of eternity melting away with her straightforward and uncoerced apology. "It's the doctor. She, and so many like her, should never be able to practice medicine. It's becoming clearer that there are more mediocre to bad physicians than good ones." I applied lotion to my right leg, in no small part because in case my skin became less dry over the coming weeks, I would have something else to credit besides the doctor's asinine advice. I was tempted not to drink any more water at all, except I was pretty sure that dying of dehydration would be less than satisfactory revenge.

"Luckily the kids have a good pediatrician." Sarah sat down on her makeup stool. "What's our next step?"

"I've showered. Let me toss on some clothes, and then we'll take the kids someplace. Everyone has been feeling cooped up. I hear Rockport is nice. It's a Tuesday. How crowded can it be?" I ran a hand through my wet and recently shorn hair with the relief that came from having at least one thing in my life that was easy. "Hair's done."

"It still amazes me how different our getting ready routines are." She shook her head but laughed. "And, you know I wasn't talking about our plans for today."

"Correct, but I need time to process. In the meantime, let's take the kids and your mom to see the ocean. It's seventy degrees. In March! Is there a better way to spend a day? I'm willing to bet we can find an ice cream stand in one of the seaside towns. Not sure I can find cows to provide entertainment while we indulge, though."

She snorted. "You're never going to let me live that down. As for the plans today, you had me at ocean. I'll call Mom now and tell her we'll be over soon."

CHAPTER SEVEN

Sarah sat in the passenger seat as I steered the SUV along the coastal road. I crouched over the steering wheel to peer at the sky, but my eyes were continually pulled to all of the power lines along the side of the road.

"Is all of New England like this, do you think?" I asked, pointing to the thick black wires looping from pole to pole.

"Not sure. It's weird to see. We didn't have this in Fort Collins, right?" She didn't sound entirely certain, and I felt much the same.

"It's funny. We've only been gone for a year or so, but it's hard to recall. My gut says no because it's shocking to see all these lines and electric poles every one hundred feet. It's 2021. How do they keep the power on during storms?"

"Considering we've lost power a few times in the past three months, I'm guessing not very well." Sarah had her trusty phone in her hand. "According to a news article, ninety-seven percent of the power lines in Fort Collins are underground, so we're not losing our minds."

"That's debatable, but it's good to know we weren't imagining things. Given the evidence of why we keep losing power, I think I need to stock up on more ice to ensure we don't lose all our food every time the wind blows."

"Half our freezer is already stuffed with frozen-water-filled Tupperware as it is." Sarah groaned.

"We lost power for almost twenty-four hours last month, right after I'd stocked up the food supply. Hundreds of dollars worth." This wasn't the first time Sarah had offered some commentary on my Operation Save Freezer quest.

"At this rate, next time it goes out, all we'll have to lose is ice."

Ignoring Sarah's annoyingly astute observation, I eyed the sagging lines from pole to pole. Some of the lines were going through tree branches. I made a mental note to freeze more containers of water. One couldn't be too prepared, and naysayers be damned.

"Oh, I didn't see what that green sign back there said." Sarah sat up in the seat and hooked a thumb over her shoulder. "I'm pretty certain it had the word *historical*. Pull off here, and let's find out."

I did as instructed, grinning. "You know me and history."

"I'm fully aware," she said sweetly. "I want it noted we're not stopping for me or the children, dear."

"Aw, you either want me to know you love me no matter what, or you're angling for a sticker on your good girl chart."

"Can't it be both?" She gave my thigh a gentle squeeze.

There was a parking lot off the side of the road where a handful of masked people were returning to their cars, their arms laden with musical instruments. Not the type you'd find in a marching band or orchestra, but much more exotic-looking. Like the ones hippies would play.

"I wonder if they were doing a drum circle or something." Sarah sat up to get a better view of the happenings in the lot.

I shrugged, waiting for an older woman to finish storing her drum and climb into her vehicle before I could open my car door. It took a lot longer than it seemed like it should. Not that we were in a rush, and I didn't think it right to yell at a woman who had forty-something years on me to hurry the fuck up so I could history-nerd out. Not to mention, Sarah's mom was in the back with the kids. Ever since Rose got hearing aids, she didn't miss much, putting more pressure on me to curb my Lizzie outbursts that not many appreciated.

When the other people in the lot disappeared into their cars, we started getting the kiddos out, doing our best to control the twins, who wanted to race toward the water despite the road we had to cross. Not to mention, the thought of letting them climb the rocky shore all on their own stopped my nervous-Nelly heart.

"Hold on, Ollie. We're almost ready." I gripped her chubby hand, not wanting to squeeze it too hard but also desiring to keep her from breaking free. Considering she wasn't quite five yet, her grip-strength was impressive. With my other hand, I held onto Fred, who was looking skyward at the seagulls squawking overhead and not putting up a struggle at all.

Right when I sensed Ollie was about to lose it, Sarah finished getting Calvin out, Rose grabbed Demi's hand, and we were good to go.

The grass was more brown than green as we crossed a small field to a dirt pathway near the shore. The ocean was ahead of us, waves crashing angrily, and while there was an opening to head down to the beach, a sharp wind blasted our faces. I warily eyed the rocky route, calculating the odds of maneuvering all of us safely down. My unscientific assessment put it right between highly unlikely and completely impossible.

Sarah must have been of the same mind because without consulting any of us, she started down the path to our left toward a large boulder. From this distance, roughly fifty yards away, I could see a sign by the rock. It had the look of something important, probably sharing why this particular patch of land was significant. It wasn't unusual to stumble upon signs like this in Massachusetts since the state brimmed with history, and naturally, any time I saw one, I was dying to know more.

Much to my surprise, Ollie didn't put up a major fight about not climbing over the rocks to the shoreline, but she was a Colorado kid, and the ocean wasn't in her blood. The centennial state was landlocked, and we hadn't explored the seaside much given the majority of our time in Massachusetts had been spent in lockdown. There was also a possibility that Ollie's eyesight wasn't great, so I added a mental note to mention that to Sarah later.

We made it to the rock, and I squinted, wishing I'd worn my sunglasses with my baseball hat, but I hadn't mastered not fogging them up while also sporting a mask.

Sarah, who could manage sunglasses and a cloth covering over her mouth like a pro, took pity on my lesser abilities and read the sign. "'On this site in 1623, a company of fishermen and farmers from Dorchester, England, under the direction of the Reverend John White founded the Massachusetts Bay Colony.'"

"Really?" I asked, excitement coursing through me.

"Apparently so." Her tone was completely flat. Unlike me, Sarah's enthusiasm for historical trivia was at basement level.

"This is quite a find, isn't it, kiddos?" I peered down at the twins, hoping they would catch my excitement by being in close proximity. Freddie was smiling at me, but Ollie was staring over her shoulder at something in the distance. Narrowing my eyes, I could make out the faintest hint of playground equipment. How had she seen it? At least, this meant I could scratch having Ollie's eyes checked off my mental to-do list.

Sarah must've noticed the playground at the same time because she gave me a *sorry Charlie* look. "I'm sure they would've found your rock very interesting, but it's hard to compete with slides."

We started for the playground, and I tried to be brave. For me, this meant doing my best not to look over my shoulder and cast longing glances at my unexplored historical monument. I said tried, not succeeded. I ended up peeking more than once, each time heaving a sorrowful sigh. Still, I thought I'd been relatively subtle until I caught my wife shaking her head, her expression making it clear she'd witnessed the whole thing.

"Once we get the kids playing, you can go back on your own," Sarah promised.

There was more pep in my step now, and I felt like a dark cloud had been lifted from my day. "You really are the best wife on the planet."

"And you are the biggest baby when you can't read a bunch of boring facts about dead people. It's entirely possible I'm doing this for my benefit because I really don't want to hear you complain for the rest of the day."

Rose chuckled.

"I'm not that bad." A sudden rush of doubt prompted me to add, "Am I?"

"I was teasing. Honest. I know how much you like this stuff." The way she said it left little doubt that though she didn't share my interest, I hadn't been that bad. Or maybe I really was that bad, but I'd already had a terrible day, and she didn't want to add yet another thing to my list of daily complaints because I was the type to keep mental track of shittery.

That didn't stop me from pressing my luck. "We should have snapped a family photo in front of it."

"Oh, honestly, Lizzie." Sarah made a sound that was part laugh and part groan. "Okay. We will on our way back. I promise."

"Is the temperature dropping?" A blast of wind practically sliced through me.

"Perhaps you shouldn't wear shorts so early in the season." She seemed overly amused by the goosebumps spreading across my body.

I still proclaimed, "No can do. Once I pull my shorts out after the first nice day, I can't go back to pants. Life is too short for pants strangling me. Not until November."

"November!"

Rose tsked, but that was her only contribution to the conversation.

"Fingers crossed. Look, Ollie. Swings!" Okay, I used Ollie as a diversion from the shorts-pants argument because we'd been circling back to this like a marital spat merry-go-round.

True to her word, once all the kids were busy on the playground, I got the go-ahead from Sarah that it was safe to depart. I practically skipped all the way back to the monument. I snapped a few photos and worked my way around to the other side, where I spied a trail through a split in the rock formation. Without taking a moment to consider whether it was a good idea to do so, I headed up. Fortunately for me, it was more of a gentle slope and less of a mountain climbing experience, and I was soon at the top.

The view of the Atlantic Ocean momentarily took my breath away. It seemed endless and churning with power as waves pummeled the rocks along the coast. What had it been like for the early settlers to climb aboard a ship, travelling to a place they'd never been before? They'd had no way of knowing what they would find in the so-called new world, and for many, it hadn't ended well. Would I have been up for the challenge?

I suspected I would have been one of the folks who'd opted to stay behind. Frankly, the bravery of embarking on such a quest put my own efforts to find out whether or not I was autistic to shame. After all, even if I did have the A-word, there was zero chance I would be eaten by a shark because of it.

After taking one last look at the water, I turned to head back to my family. Having established I wasn't as brave as I might've liked, I was especially grateful for them, my rock in the turbulent seas of life.

CHAPTER EIGHT

"Over there!" With a level of enthusiasm usually reserved for spotting a hundred-dollar bill on the ground, Sarah waved to a parking space. "I thought for sure we weren't going to find one."

"I had no idea Rockport was such a popular place," I said, my nerves frazzled from the long hunt. "Otherwise, I would have suggested staying in Gloucester after lunch."

I put my blinker on to let the drivers behind me know I needed to parallel park, but when I started to back into the slot, the car behind me attempted careening around our SUV, nearly wiping out an oncoming car. Both drivers honked ferociously while jabbing their middle fingers at me. How the hell was this my fault?

"My blinker is on, fudge holes!" I muttered, knowing that at such a low volume, and with the windows up, there was no way they would hear me. Still, it made me feel a smidge better. I peeked at Sarah. "How do they expect me to park?"

"I doubt they care at all what you are trying to do, only how it inconveniences them," Sarah explained. "I believe the actual term for them is Massholes."

I chuckled, straightening the wheels to pull forward. "That's funny. Did you just come up with that?"

"No. It's something I found in the Massachusetts Transplant Facebook group. I learned that nugget and that Massachusetts has some of the worst drivers in the country. I think Boston ranked as number two."

"I've been noticing that." I finished parking the vehicle. "All I can say is I'd hate to drive in whatever city was ranked number one. Now, let's figure out how to pay for the privilege of leaving our car here. Sometimes, I really miss Fort Collins and all the free parking." I scouted the street in front of me and then over my shoulder. "I don't see any meters, so I'm betting there's some sort of fancy app I'll have to download."

I carefully checked my blind spot before opening the door and stepping out into the road. I sprinted around the car like it was the final meters of a race just to deny a Masshole the pleasure of mowing me down. Were they always this angry, or was it a result of COVID? Time would tell, I guessed.

A few car lengths away, there was a blue parking kiosk, a relief to see since at least it meant I didn't have to figure out a way to pay with my phone like in some of the other towns I'd seen. That still didn't mean it was easy. By the time I read halfway through the directions, Sarah had gotten out of the car and stood next to me. Now, she was reading the same directions, which was reassuring, even if I didn't want to let on. The truth was, I wasn't known for figuring things out on my own, and what I'd read so far hadn't made much sense.

"Insert your card," she instructed.

I did as I was told.

Then I removed the card quickly as directed, but when I tried to add more time, the machine had already spit out a ticket for only one hour.

Sarah eyed the paper. "I'm not sure where we went wrong,

but let's try again. It'll take us an hour to get the kids out of the car." She was joking, obviously, but not by much.

I went through the same motions and got another ticket for one hour for my efforts. "Do you think we can place both in the window next to each other and call it done? Technically, we paid for two hours."

"They're time-stamped," Sarah said, pointing from one ticket to the next. "The second attempt only gained us a minute."

"Massholes," I muttered, inserting my card again. This time, I was able to bump the time up to four hours, although for the life of me, I couldn't figure out what I'd done differently aside from frantically pressing every button on the screen before the ticket printed.

"Great job, Lizzie!" Sarah shook my arm as if I'd crossed the Boston Marathon finish line.

"I'm pretty sure that's intentional," I complained, grumpy over my wasted money, as Sarah squirted sanitizer into my right palm. "How many people pay for an hour when they actually need more time and have to start all over again?"

Sarah shrugged, letting the injustice go without another thought. Which may or may not have been her way of avoiding having to break it to me that I was the only one to be so afflicted.

I growled under my breath, trying to dismiss the injustice, but it was harder for the likes of me. I hated being cheated, even if I was only out a couple of dollars. It was the principle of it that festered like a pimple about to explode.

"Ice cream!" Ollie screamed, remembering the bribe Sarah had made when we practically had to pull her off one of the swings at the park.

"Yes," I said, amazed at her selective memory skills. She would remember ice cream for days but instantly forget anything she didn't want to do, like putting away her toys.

"Let's get everyone out of the car and seek out some ice cream, Ollie Dollie."

Ollie, Fred, and Demi trotted out of the car pretty easily, and Sarah successfully maneuvered the sleeping Calvin from his car seat to the stroller without waking him. That in itself was cause for celebration, which meant maybe I should order two scoops today.

"Everyone seems to be heading in that direction." Rose pointed over my shoulder.

"Let's roll, then."

We ended up on a street that was clearly tourist central given the large quantity of T-shirt places, candy shops, and a handful of restaurants with big red lobsters painted on the windows. However, given it wasn't summer yet, not all of the establishments were open, and that included the ice cream stands. This didn't bode well for a day without one of Olivia's epic meltdowns. My body tensed immediately.

Sarah gave me a worried look, but I trudged on, feeling in my bones we'd find something if we kept looking. When it came to the kids, I did absolutely everything to make them happy, even if that meant ordering ice cream to go from a restaurant at an exorbitant price, which would sting less than the parking ticket robbery, even if that only amounted to losing two bucks. Don't ask why because my brain is a mystery to me.

As we got closer to the end of the street, which incidentally was also where the ocean started, I caught a glimpse of a tourist shop that had an ice cream window on the side of the building.

"Victory!" I put my hand out for Ollie to high-five, which she did with relish, leaving my palm slightly red. Not that she noticed.

Fred gave me a much gentler version, and Demi simply responded by giggling. Calvin was zonked out in his stroller.

"How is he still asleep?" I commented to Sarah with

genuine amazement. "Ollie chanted the words *ice cream* almost the entire way here."

Sarah shrugged. "So far, he hasn't seemed like the biggest fan of the stuff or of Massachusetts, really."

"Cal might be the first kid I know who can't be bribed with ice cream." Rose leaned down to admire the sleeping toddler.

Sarah was too busy reading the flavor options to respond. "Let's get the twins cotton candy."

"A scoop each?"

"No. They'll share a cup."

"Why do you hate Fred?" I whispered to her.

She shot me a nasty look. "Ollie will share."

I held my still smarting hand in the air. "How can I say this politely? She gets overzealous and can be forceful."

Sarah inspected my hand and then our daughter, who was rubbing her hands together and looking more devilish than angelic. "Okay. I'll share cotton candy with Ollie. You and Fred will get—"

"Cotton candy." My desire for two scoops evaporated as I spoke. That sounded like the worst flavor ever.

"But, you love chocolate and peanut butter."

"I think Fred would prefer cotton candy." I gave myself a mental pat on the back for being such a selfless parent.

To reinforce that I was right, Fred moved his head up and down. Damn. Now there was no way I could back out of it and order chocolate peanut butter swirl instead.

"I'll have Neapolitan with Demi." Rose regarded Demi, who nodded eagerly.

Sarah placed the order, while Rose and I steered the kids to a free bench that technically belonged to a hot dog joint, but it didn't seem to be open for the season yet. Given the half-closed status of the town, I was amazed to see a fair bit of tourists wandering the street, enjoying the spring sunshine and being out of the house after one of the worst winters in our lifetimes.

"Will you be back in the classroom in the fall?" Rose rolled Calvin's stroller back and forth.

"I'm not sure yet," I answered, "but it's looking pretty likely. I've missed being in the classroom. It's been a struggle to keep students, not to mention me, engaged over Zoom."

She nodded her head. "They're calling it Zoom fatigue."

"I'm getting pretty tired of all of this sh-shittake."

Sarah carried the three cups of ice cream over to the table, and I rushed to help her in order to prevent one of them from falling to the ground. I was still smarting from the parking machine banditry and refused to have to pay twice for the same ice cream, too.

My eyes nearly bugged out of my head when I saw the cotton candy scoops were a sickly shade of pink, blue, and purple, but Freddie plunged his spoon in as soon as it hit the table, taking a bite so big it was a wonder he didn't instantly freeze his brain. When we'd shared chocolate and peanut butter days before, he hadn't been nearly so enthusiastic.

Ollie was already on her second bite, her chin dripping with sickening colors. It looked like a circus had melted on her face.

"It's the equivalent of bugs flying into a zapper," I said to Sarah as she used both hands to hold the cup for Ollie, who was forcefully digging into the frozen concoction to scoop out the largest bite.

Calvin stirred in his stroller.

"Hey there, buddy. Just in time for ice cream." I pulled him onto my lap. "It's funny. Well, no, that isn't the right word. Perhaps odd, but when you think about the fact we've been living in lockdown for half his life. He hasn't been out of the house this long for ages."

Calvin yawned, but he was perking up quickly, eyeing the goodies on the table.

"Should I see if he wants a bite?" I asked. The stuff was

disgusting, so I couldn't imagine he would, but the other kids seemed to love it.

"Why not? Now that we're opening back up, I can finally make the kiddos dentist appointments. Us, too." Sarah was joking about the dentist part, but it was completely true that cotton candy ice cream looked like cavities in the making.

Calvin was more awake, so I scooped out a tiny bite and offered it to him.

At first, I thought it was going to be another no-go, but after poking his tongue out for a taste, he placed his mouth all the way around the spoon. After he finished, he gave a wide smile saying, "Yummy!"

"Why do I suddenly feel like we've been denying the children real ice cream goods all these years?" I asked, marveling at how quickly the cotton candy goo was sliding down their gullets. "How can they possibly like this stuff?"

Before I could talk her out of it, Sarah took a tiny taste. "It's not as bad as I thought. You should give it a try."

"I can't get past the color." I looked mournfully at Rose and Demi's cup of Neapolitan.

Demi, who didn't miss much, offered me a bite.

"Aw, thanks, my little Demitasse!"

The twins chatted excitedly using words that we had started referring to as their twin-speak, since only the two of them understood what the other said. Okay, that wasn't entirely true. Demi would toss in an occasional word, so perhaps it was simply kid-speak. Either way, it always filled my heart with joy that our children not only got along but engaged in animated conversations.

Sarah ate more of the cotton candy, swishing it around in her mouth the way you do with wine at a tasting. "It grows on you."

The word *grows* triggered a memory of that blasted scale at

A WOMAN UNHINGED

the doctor's office. "After being weighed this morning, it's probably for the best I don't have any."

Rose grunted, and I had to wonder if that was her way of saying she had noticed I put on ten pounds or if she was referring to her own bathroom scale experience. The fact that most of the world was experiencing what the news had started calling the *COVID Twenty* didn't make me feel any better about it.

"This is family day. Calories don't count." Sarah held a spoon out for me to try the cotton candy monstrosity. "Come on. You can never say no to me."

"You aren't playing fair." I could have said more about when I could and could not say no to my wife, but we had four sets of little ears listening, not to mention my mother-in-law. Defeated, I accepted the bite, regretting it immediately as I wiped my tongue on a flimsy paper napkin. "You tricked me!"

"It's not that bad," Sarah insisted. "I'm almost liking it now."

I continued wiping my tongue with the napkin, avoiding Sarah's eyes. Desperate for a change in topic, I said, "This is a cute town."

"I'm loving all these sea towns. Now that the weather is improving, we need to explore more."

A yellow sign caught my eyes, and I read the words slowly: *Cat X-Ing*. "Ex-ing. Is that the Massachusetts way of spelling *xing*?" I asked, pronouncing the X in the word like I would xylophone. I chuckled. "Goodness knows they don't know the rules of the road, so maybe spelling isn't their thing, either. Or stopping for pedestrians."

Sarah followed my eyes. "You mean crossing?"

"No. Xing." I blinked to clear my eyes and then read the sign again. "X-Ing is short for crossing? What about pedestrian xings?"

There was a stunned look on Sarah's face before she was

67

able to get out, "Are you telling me, all this time, you weren't calling them xings as a joke? I always thought it was one of your corny go-tos to mock something?"

I couldn't focus on the word corny at that moment, nor stop to question what else I did that fell into that category. Instead, I was zeroing in on the one thing blowing my mind. "Xing isn't a word? Not at all?"

"Nope."

"Xing!" Ollie punched my arm, bringing tears to my eyes.

"I swear she's getting too smart for her own good. Not to mention zealous." I massaged my arm.

"No hitting, Ollie," Sarah admonished, but it didn't come out too harshly since Sarah was doing her best not to laugh at Ollie's timing. Besides, she was already engrossed in another conversation with Fred and Demi. Sarah perked up. "Shall we seek out fudge? This seems like the type of place that will have fabulous fudge."

"We just ate ice cream," I protested, although to be technical about it, they had eaten ice cream. I had not.

"There's always room for fudge." Rose was deadly serious, and I was leaning toward believing her scale hadn't delivered bad news like mine, which meant she had been commenting about my weight gain.

I looked down at my gut. "That's my problem. Now that my thyroid is sorta functioning the way it should, I have to worry about calories. I've never had to do that in my life until now."

"We'll do it together but starting tomorrow. I want fudge, and I have it on good authority there are no calories in fudge." Sarah gave me her *please don't say no* smile while I added *shop for exercise equipment* to my mental to-do list and chalked up my xing mix-up to the growing evidence that I was, indeed, autistic. I wasn't for sure convinced quite yet, but when it came to the dreaded A-word, it wasn't looking good.

CHAPTER NINE

After my Zoom class on Tuesday afternoon, Willow found me in the library. Which is to say, the room in which I did all of my work but wasn't allowed to call my office. I still didn't understand it, but it was a newish rule, so I did my best to comply because I'd learned being in the proverbial doghouse meant no sexy time with my wife.

"Got a second?" Willow asked.

I sat back in my chair and threaded my fingers behind my head. "Sure."

"How was class?"

That was a red flag. I knew she hadn't come in here to chat about my work, but I didn't want to call her out, either, so I responded, "Oh, fabulous. These are great times to be teaching about the rise of Hitler and all the warning signs the international community missed back in the 1930s about how bad the Nazis would be for the world. A lot sounds disconcertingly familiar today. I never used to think that, but after January sixth, it's getting harder and harder to avoid the comparisons."

"I bet." She looked around nervously, almost as if she was expecting Hitler's ghost to pop out from behind the furniture.

"What's wrong?"

"Maddie and I had a big fight." She fiddled with one of her earrings, eyes focused on the carpet.

My arms fell, and I straightened in my seat. "I'm sorry. Do you want to talk about it?" Getting stuck in the middle of their argument didn't sound like a good situation, but how could I not ask when she came in here to talk to me? Clearly, she wanted to vent. Why she'd chosen me was a complete mystery.

"She's been working a lot of hours." Willow slumped down in the seat across from me, her hands gripping the arms of the chair.

"Yeah," I said slowly, not entirely convinced this was the problem Willow was making it out to be. "With everyone spending the majority of their hours at home, many are desperate to give their spaces a fresh look. COVID has been a boon for her interior design business."

"Which is great."

That had been my thought, too, but Willow's tone was harsh enough that even I picked up on the fact that she did not actually think this was great.

"I sense there's a *but* coming," I prompted.

"Not really a *but*." Willow's gaze dropped to her lap momentarily before she slowly raised her eyes to mine when I didn't say anything. This was a trick I'd learned from my therapist who pulled it on me more times than I cared to admit when I needed to unload but wasn't sure where to begin.

I motioned for her to rip off the bandage.

"I thought it'd be nice for us to get a place of our own so when we do have time together, it could be just the two of us. It's not that I don't like living here. I love the kids, and there's always something to do. It's just alone time is needed. Not to mention, it'd be nice for her to work out of a home office that wasn't also our bedroom."

"I see." I was trying to curb my excitement. If Willow could persuade Maddie to get a place of their own, then it'd be Sarah, the kids, and me. It wouldn't be quiet because with four kids, a dog and cat, silence wasn't on the menu until all of them moved out of the house. The kids, that is. The dog and cat were tolerable, and I certainly hoped Sarah had no plans to go. Reducing our occupancy rate by two adults would give me more breathing room, of which I was in desperate need. I had to tread lightly, though. "She doesn't want to?"

"She's conflicted."

"Did she say about what?"

"Demi."

This wasn't a surprise. Maddie had been engaged to my brother, who was Demi's father before he gave up parental rights when sent to prison for financial shenanigans. Deep down, I suspected Maddie still carried a torch for Peter. In fact, it was Peter who had encouraged me to ensure Maddie moved out of Colorado because he wanted her to move on with her life. Was Willow worried about the same thing?

I didn't want to know but felt compelled to ask, "Is it simply because of Demi?"

Please say yes. I held my breath. The other option would be extremely awkward to discuss with Willow. How could I say, once you fall for a Petrie, you're stuck? I mean, I hoped it was true in my case because thinking of life without Sarah sounded so very lonely and miserable. My brother, on the other hand, was hardly worth so much angst. Maddie deserved better.

"I keep asking myself that very question."

Well, crap.

"Does that mean you haven't asked her?"

Again, Willow shook her head, and it brought home how alike we were. While our brains purred with insecurities, they also ground to a halt when it came to asking the tough questions needed to unearth the answers we were desperate for. At least that was the case with me, and I suspected with Willow as well, which had to be why she'd come to me instead of Sarah. My wife was the type who would make Willow march straight over to Maddie and ask her outright.

"Yeah." I sighed, knowing I should be more like Sarah but also knowing I couldn't be. "I imagine hearing a certain answer would be devastating."

"I'm hoping it's all the reasons that make sense, the big ones like I'm out of a job. There's still a pandemic. Housing prices are skyrocketing, and finding something close enough to stay in daily contact with Demi will be difficult." Willow ticked everything off on her fingers, giving me a pretty good idea she'd been running through the list nonstop in that head of hers.

It was hard not to burst into laughter because all of those thoughts had also occurred to me, but I knew laughing would be the worst reaction in the moment.

"So, you've been looking for places?" My inner grump wanted to do a victory dance around the room, perhaps naked, but not with Willow present. Who was I kidding? I wasn't the *naked dancing* type. Or even the *clothed dancing* type. Maybe a heel click?

"I've been checking out some options on Zillow," she replied, "but nothing serious."

I bobbed my head, remembering how Sarah had made me look at houses when we knew we were moving to Massachusetts. "That's a start," I said.

"When did you know you wanted to be with Sarah? Like, forever?"

"Probably the first time I looked into her eyes, but my brain conspired against me, and I did everything I could to blow it up right out of the gate. Just the word *commitment* sent me into a tizzy." I shook about in my chair.

"I think Maddie is your long-lost twin."

That idea slammed into my brain, not for the first time, but I conveniently forgot certain facts I didn't care to keep at the forefront of my brain. For as long as I'd known Maddie, she'd made questionable choices with significant others. She'd been engaged twice that I knew of, once to Peter, my eldest brother, and the other time to my stepbrother, Gabe, whom I didn't know about until four years ago because my dad had a secret family while married to my mother. To make matters worse, Maddie had also dated Courtney, who, at the time, had been engaged to Kit, Peter's brother-in-law. Part of me had thought it was the Petrie curse, the convoluted family dynamics that made our family tree look more like a conspiracy chart.

Was Willow right, though? Not that Maddie and I had been separated at birth, since I was doing every bit of mental jujitsu to keep that thought from penetrating my brain. Because, ew.

But I'd always wondered about Maddie's relationship choices, and I hadn't even mentioned Doug the Weatherman. I never understood how she could get the hots for a dude named Doug who lied for a living. I long suspected Maddie wasn't the settling down type, and she chose people in her life who were the worst possible forever mates to reinforce her commitment-phobe tendencies. Was she so far gone on that path that even when she found the right one, she couldn't right the ship?

Over the past few months, I had started to believe Willow was Maddie's Sarah. The woman who could change everything for the better. Maddie had told me as much at one point. Was Maddie about to wreck her chances for true happiness out of fear or something even more nefarious buried deep down?

I wished I could consult Sarah about how to tackle this thorny problem, but I couldn't exactly call for a time-out in my conversation with Willow to get an emergency consultation. While I cheered for Willow and Maddie to be happy, I also desired to have fewer people under one roof. Not wanting to jeopardize my chance for solitude, and in no hurry to get into the discussion of whether Maddie was the type to settle down, all I could think to say was, "For your sake, I hope that isn't the case."

"What can I do?"

Move to a new apartment and sort it out there?

"Be patient. Maddie's track record in this department isn't great. That's probably weighing on her."

Willow's expression was forlorn. "Understandably so with Demi pulling Maddie in two different directions."

"Poor Demi drew the short straw with both parents. You never met Tie, but she was the worst type of mother to bring a life into the world. Sarah, Maddie, and I want to ensure she has the best of everything else, and none of us knows how to handle certain questions when she gets older."

"Like what?" Willow asked.

"Like telling her she's adopted and that Uncle Peter is actually her father. Look, I know it's not easy to give the woman you love space to deal with emotions, but pressing her before she's ready will only blow things up prematurely. I recommend you talk to Sarah. She has a lot of experience dealing with an idiot." I pounded my chest with my palm in case there was any doubt as to the identity of said idiot. "The woman's a saint."

Willow nodded, but I sensed my poor attempt to perk her up had made the situation much worse. Feeling like a total failure, I said, "I'm excited about recording our first podcast episode next week."

"Yeah, me too," Willow replied but without a trace of the enthusiasm she professed to have. I'd definitely made things worse. As she got up to leave, I wanted to jab my pen into my eye.

When the door closed, I let out an exasperated sigh. "Way to go, idiot."

I'd completely bombed at giving advice, brought Willow zero comfort—or possibly increased her anxiety—and worst of all, now they would never move out.

Another thought niggled at my brain. Willow's comment about needing alone time with Maddie. I related to that on two fronts. I needed moments with just Sarah. Also, I needed Lizzie time, hence my camp chair in the closet. The thought causing my brain to short circuit was: where did my wife go when she needed Sarah time?

Somehow, I'd never questioned this before, but now that I had, it struck me what a problem it was. Unfortunately, I didn't have a solution.

CHAPTER TEN

EARLY ON SATURDAY MORNING—AND I'm not sure how to say this without being completely blunt—I was on the toilet. There was a slight chill in the air, and I grabbed a hoodie that sat on the bench near the commode. I slipped it over my head, and that was when things went south.

As I attempted to put my arms through the holes, I realized the sweatshirt was on backward. Not wanting to remove it completely, because that seemed like a wasted effort, I tried rotating the hoodie. It really shouldn't have been that hard. Or so I thought. The damn thing became hopelessly entangled with the collar of my button-up shirt, tightening uncomfortably around my neck.

For as long as I can remember, I've never liked anything near the vicinity of my neck. At all of the graduation ceremonies where I had to wear full academic regalia, every single photo shows me tugging the hood portion off my neck as if to prevent being strangled.

Now, it seemed like I was truly being asphyxiated by my own clothing, and panic started to set in.

Think, Lizzie!

I struggled to move my left arm, but I couldn't get it past the point of the snarl around my neck. I encountered the same result with my right arm. This is the point where I began to fear I was going to die while sitting on the toilet, like Elvis.

My heart rate ticked upward, straight past panic to the rarely encountered *bring in the helicopter to save my life* level. Did first responders have a sweatshirt jaws of life?

Frantically, I tried to use brute force to free my head, but this only triggered the fabric to constrict further, reminding me of those bamboo finger traps that were popular in the fourth grade. I never liked them back then, either. Way too tight. No matter how hard I tried to relax my mind enough to remember to push my fingers inward, not outward, I never managed to free myself from them without tearing the tube to shreds.

Naturally, it was only at a time like this that I would even remember the trick for escaping finger traps, and it held absolutely no relevance to my current conundrum. I know because I tried to think of any way to apply the principle to my sweatshirt, to no avail. Finally, I resorted to tearing at it, Incredible Hulk style, but my efforts to split the thick fabric netted zero results.

"Fuck, fuck, fuck!"

"Are you okay?" Sarah spoke from the other side of the door, and I could hear that quite familiar edge to her tone, the one that said she knew I was in trouble and was afraid to find out how.

"You're up?" The words came out like an extra high-pitched impersonation of Snow White as I did my best to sound like there was nothing to see on my side of the door. Which, actually, was close to the truth. The way the hoodie was stuck around my face, I was essentially blind.

"Yes. What's going on? You sound funny. Like you're muffled. Do you have a cold?" There was a touch of panic in her voice as she suggested it, and for good reason. This wasn't the time to present any cold symptoms, or everyone immediately assumed you had COVID.

Not wanting to stress her out, I said as reassuringly as possible, "No cold. Nothing's wrong with me. Not at all."

"Then why do you sound like you're drowning?"

She wasn't buying it, and I wasn't surprised. It'd always been impossible to fool Sarah, who had an uncanny sixth sense when it came to discovering me in bad situations. I considered staying silent to save my pride, but who was I kidding? After the scrapes Sarah had witnessed over the years, I had no pride left.

"I'm stuck."

"On the toilet or in it?" To her credit, she kept her voice judgement free, and there was a good chance she truly thought either one of those possibilities was legit. All things considered, it wasn't like I was in a position to say *Don't be silly*, as if what I had managed to get myself into was any better than the options she'd presented. But when had that ever stopped me from overreacting?

"Of course not," I shrieked. "I'm stuck in my hoodie!"

There was a sort of choking cough that had to have been the sound of Sarah holding back laughter. "Do you want me to come in to help?"

"No." If I could've crossed my arms, I would have. "This is how I want to leave this world. I'm ready."

The door opened, and her earlier restraint gave way to a burst of laughter, but she quickly curbed it. "How in the world…? Hold on."

The fabric started to move, and I flinched, instinctively pulling away.

"I'm trying to help," Sarah scolded, "so hold still."

"Sorry," I said with a whimper. "But I can't see, and it's getting hard to breathe."

"It's like you're expecting me to hurt you or something."

She said it with a hint of disbelief that told me she suspected the thought had actually crossed my mind.

And yeah. It had.

"It's no secret I can be pretty annoying, and if you were trying to kill me, this would be an embarrassing way to go. I'd have to give you extra points for capitalizing on such a humiliating predicament." I couldn't help but laugh, though I immediately realized the error and stopped as quickly as I could, not wanting to jeopardize what precious little oxygen I had left.

"I wouldn't say you're annoying, but you do have a strange sense of humor." Sarah clucked her tongue, and something loosened from my throat, just enough to give me hope. "I think I've finally figured out what's going on and how to fix it, even if I have no idea how you got to this point."

True to her word, Sarah soon had me free. As quickly as it had gotten tangled, the hoodie was back in its proper place, and I was able to get my arms through the holes. My eyes misted with relief.

"T-thanks," I stuttered, inhaling deeply to fill my lungs.

"Sometimes, I have to remind myself you have a PhD." Sarah smiled down at me, flattening my hair, which I was sure stuck up in random patches. Even on good days, my cowlicks gave me crazy hairdos.

"Me too," I confessed. "I'm kind of an idiot."

"A very lovable one." She kissed the top of my head.

"Promise not to tell anyone about this."

"First rule of the bathroom. The shit stays here."

I burst into laughter. "Well done. Have you been holding onto that one for a crisis like this?"

"Oh, yeah. It's been keeping me up at night, but I knew, with you, it was only a matter of time until this happened. Now, if you're done, I need to pee."

"Don't rush me! Who knows what damage that'll cause?" I

looked up into her gorgeous eyes, grinning. "But to show my appreciation for saving me, I'll get Calvin up."

As if on cue, Calvin started to cry. After pulling my jeans back up without any additional mishap. I leapt into action. Another crazy morning in the Petrie household had begun.

Later that morning, I was curled up on the couch in the library with Calvin, Freddie, and Demi, reading *The Gruffalo* aloud. Sarah came in with Ollie in tow, and while Sarah settled on the couch opposite us, she seemed to be tenser than normal, like she wanted to say something but didn't want to interrupt. Perhaps Sarah's mood was related to Ollie running around both couches with her hands in the air, happily screaming. Luckily, we finished the last line, and as soon as I shut the book, Fred and Demi joined Ollie in her antics.

Anxiety pinging through my veins, I looked frantically at Sarah, who simply raised a *what can you do* shoulder while wearing a forced serene expression, because she had that ability to appear calm in most situations.

"I think we need to get the kids outside for some fresh air and exercise." I smothered one of my ears with my palm.

"That's why I came in," Sarah said. "Mom booked us a walking slot at Tower Hill. It's a bit of a drive, but they're doing a fairy hunt."

"Hunting?" I sliced my free hand through the air to indicate absolutely not. "You know I'm completely against hunting." The other word invaded my brain. "Not to mention fairies don't exist, so how can we hunt them? I'm really not following."

Sarah gave me her *you're so fucking clueless* smile, which at this point in our lives together had pretty much become her default expression, come to think of it. "I'm no more in favor of hunting than you are. The hunt isn't real, and neither are the fairies, by the way. They've placed three hundred statues of fairies on the grounds, and we get to wander around and *find* them."

She made quote marks around the word *find*, and I bobbed my head as the entire enterprise began to make a lot more sense. "I'm game, and I bet I spy the most!"

"I wonder where our kids get their competitive streaks from." Sarah crossed her arms. This was probably meant to punish me in some way, but it resulted in me getting a better glimpse of her goods, so I was all for it. She followed my eyes, quickly catching on. "You can be such a pig sometimes."

"Would you rather I didn't appreciate them?" I inquired, tilting my head to one side.

She huffed but in a playful way. I think we both knew she got as much enjoyment from being admired as I did from appreciating her cleavage. Honestly, my refusing to remove my gaze from her chest was probably more for her benefit than it was for my own. I didn't get nearly enough recognition for my altruistic tendencies.

Knowing I would get a palm across the back of my head if I made this observation out loud, I dived back into the matter at hand. "About this hunt. Do we need scorecards for everyone? Color coded pens? What color do you think goes with each kid? Fred seems to like pink more than Ollie. Demi loves all shades of blue. Calvin is grumpier, so green? I'm less sure about that one. No doubt Ollie is red, though. Someone will end up bleeding because of her."

Sarah let out what I can best describe as a long-suffering sigh. "Instead of turning this into a Petrie free-for-all, why don't we go to have fun and wear out the kids?"

"But..." I failed to come up with an argument, other than competition being the cornerstone of my philosophy on life, which I knew wouldn't fly. I resorted to jutting out my bottom lip. Looking pathetic could work in a pinch.

Unmoved, she said, "How about you help me get the kiddos ready instead?"

"For what?"

"The fairy hunt. We were literally just speaking about it."

I shook my head like a cartoon character doing a double-take, my chest constricting sharply. "You want to go *today*?"

"Of course, today." She looked at her Fitbit, sighing. "We need to get everyone loaded into the car pronto." She did her mommy-clapping thing that translated to: The great mommy has spoken, so everyone move their butts.

"Why'd you book today? It's not like you can storm the beaches of Normandy without planning." My heart plummeted to my ankles. I was overwhelmed and wanted to find a place to hide. "I'm not known for spontaneity."

"Understatement of the century." Sarah took both of my hands into hers, the touch of her skin against mine making me feel instantly less shaky and on edge. "It's going to be okay, Lizzie. We're not planning a major operation. Just a simple family outing."

"I know, but I was prepared for a stay-at-home day with the kids, and now we're not doing that." Taking back a hand, I swiped it over my hair, bits of which were still poking up more than normal ever since the toilet incident that morning when I'd almost died. Didn't Sarah realize the day had already been traumatic enough without throwing an impromptu family outing into the mix?

Right then, Ollie shoved Freddie to the ground, and the usually docile twin lurched to his feet and pushed his sister onto the carpet. Both started crying, setting off Calvin, and Demi ran over and buried her face into Sarah's legs. I'd survived my earlier ordeal, but the rate these kids were going, they weren't going to make it to the end of the day intact unless we intervened. Quickly.

I pushed past my discomfort and plastered a brave look onto my face. "Okay. Let's get them into the car."

The maneuver only took thirty-seven minutes, give or take a few seconds, which was a record according to my iPhone stopwatch. I pulled out of the driveway, and two cars started to follow. "Are Maddie and Willow coming as well?"

"Yep."

"Why aren't they riding with Troy and Rose?"

"Maddie and Willow have plans later with some of Willow's friends." Sarah checked her reflection in the light-up mirror on the back of the visor.

"What plans? There's a pandemic." I flicked my right hand in the air before putting it back firmly on the steering wheel. "Will they be outside? Wear masks?"

"They didn't say, and I didn't ask." The finality underlying Sarah's words made it clear that was all there was to it as far as she was concerned. "Besides, we're driving someplace right now. It's not like you can judge them."

I did not share this sentiment.

"But… we're taking three cars. Has anyone heard of the greater threat to humanity? The one that doesn't have a vaccine to get us out of hot water." I didn't wait for Sarah to offer a guess, going immediately for the answer. "The climate crisis is going to kill all of us, and honestly, we deserve it. The way we treat this planet like it doesn't matter is horrendous."

"Why are you in a bad mood?" Sarah glanced in the back seat to see if any of the kids were listening, but Calvin was already asleep, and the rest were watching *Frozen II* for the gazillionth time.

"I'm sick and tired of no one caring about the bigger issue."

"Are you lumping me into that category?" She folded her arms in a goods-denying way, a sure sign I was skating on thin ice. I wasn't so easily deterred. It's not like I'd never broken through the ice before. In fact, I was pretty accustomed to an occasional dunk in frigid water by now. "I recycle everything that can be according to the number on the item. I've been limiting our meat intake. I've even started taking shorter showers."

"Because I stand outside with a timer!"

"Which doesn't make my showers all that relaxing, by the way."

"Would you prefer an egg timer instead of me shouting?" I hadn't considered my method of alerting her to the time.

"I'd prefer not being timed."

"I'd prefer saving the planet." I glanced in the rearview mirror. "The shower training might come in handy when we can move to Mars."

"As in the planet?" Her voice hit a high note I'd never heard from her before.

I nodded, turning my blinker on to take a right as the GPS instructed.

"Are you pulling my leg?" Sarah's look said she sure hoped so.

"No." Of course, I was serious. I'd given it plenty of thought. "This planet is fu-fudged up beyond repair."

"I don't think Mars is the answer. We're going to have to do better with this planet."

I looked in the rearview mirror at the two cars following me and felt twitchy all over. "We're off to a stellar start."

"Willow's car is electric."

"That's true." Considering Willow wasn't gainfully employed, I questioned her buying a car at all, but I had to give her credit for going the extra step for the planet. "Should we get an electric car?"

"Would it stop you from yelling at me and wanting to move to Mars?"

"I can't make any promises on that front. At least not about lecturing—"

"Is that what you call it?"

I ignored her question, which was almost certainly rhetorical, and continued my train of thought. "I think space is our best option."

"Sure, aside from not being able to breathe, plus the lack of water and gravity. Of course, you might be of the opinion those seem overrated. I would like to remind you about your unfortunate bathroom experience. You're breathing was merely uncomfortable, and you were on the verge of losing it."

"I nearly died, and you don't care!"

"It's too traumatic to dwell about." Her sarcasm was thicker than molasses. "When you really think about all the difficulties involved in moving to Mars, which clearly you've done—"

"Stop treating me like I'm a moron because you found me stuck on the toilet."

"I would never. I'm sure strangling oneself on the toilet could happen to anyone." Her shoulders shook with laughter.

"If we can't live on Mars, why are certain billionaires spending so much to explore space?"

"They're bored egomaniacs." Sarah turned in the seat, and she used her soft tone to avoid upsetting me. "Honey, please don't get your heart set on moving to Mars. It's not going to happen in our lifetime."

"What about…?" I jerked my head to the kids in the back.

Sarah peered at our darlings with her adoring mom expression. "We have to be better with this planet. For them."

My mind started to race. I tapped my fingers against the steering wheel. "I'll get a quote for solar panels on the house, price electric vehicles, and limit our single-use plastics."

"Sounds like you've got the start of a plan."

"Yeah," I agreed. I wasn't sure if Sarah actually thought I was onto something, but I decided to take her words at face value. "I'll come up with actionable steps. Like, earlier this morning when I was reading *The New York Times* on my phone, there was an ad for a reusable Q-tip. I'll get them for everyone."

"Was this before or after you got stuck in your hoodie?"

"Before. It was around three, I think."

"When all the best ideas happen."

There was enough sarcasm this time that even I couldn't take the words at face value, so I ignored her. My mind was too busy buzzing with possibilities. I had some good ideas, and that was before I'd even had a chance to google solutions. However, not that I would tell Sarah this, I wasn't ready to quit the Mars solution yet, either. There had to be a way to start over. I wasn't great at fixing, but I truly loved a blank page.

CHAPTER ELEVEN

WE ARRIVED at the botanical gardens, and as we got out of our cars, the stunning view of the hills and reservoir in the distance was enough to temporarily distract me from all the ways we were destroying the planet. In fact, the lush grounds and the flowers in bloom along the pathway to the visitor's center made it seem for a moment that all was right in the world.

Once we'd shown our e-tickets and scanned the QR code for the map, the adults all paired off with kids, and I ensured not to be partners with Maddie still unable to handle her big personality and taunts. Not that I'd said as much to Sarah, but she seemed to intuit that had been my goal ever since I confessed to her I might be the A-word. Luckily for me, Willow selected me as her adult buddy. The two of us brought up the rear with Freddie, who held onto my right hand and Willow's left.

"Fairy!" Fred dropped my hand to point to the tiny statue sticking out behind a cluster of perky yellow flowers. Somehow, I had never learned any of the flower names, a true shame because I loved them that much but could only distinguish them by color and size.

"Great spot!" I smiled down at him.

He retook my hand with an extra bounce to his step, but he let go almost immediately to point out another. While he frantically looked around to find more, I glimpsed Sarah and Maddie deep in conversation while Ollie picked up a stick off the ground to whack the dirt.

"Just what this outing was missing. An armed Olivia." I patted Fred's head after he shouted *fairy* again, keeping an eye on the situation but deciding it wasn't yet time to intervene.

"She's such a character." There was an extra bounce in Willow's step, so I assumed, or hoped, the fighting with Maddie had died down. Although, from the intensity of the conversation up ahead, I wasn't so sure.

"That's a nice way of putting it. Oh, look!" My outburst was prompted by a red cardinal, and yes, I always called them that, flying by. Sadly, before I could get my phone out of my pocket, the bird disappeared.

"Oh, too bad." Willow gave me a *better luck next time* shrug. I was not taking the disappointment nearly as calmly as she was, my determination hardening.

"Why can't they stay put like pigeons? I have a ton of snaps of them."

A grunting up ahead pulled our attention to Ollie, who was thwacking the ground with each step, sounding like a tennis player. Incidentally, she enjoyed playing tennis, and I added looking into tennis lessons for Ollie to my ever-expanding mental list, somewhere between ordering reusable Q-Tips and figuring out how to colonize Mars. I would never be able to complain I didn't have enough to keep me busy.

"If she keeps that up, it'll take us days to do this short loop." Willow looked at the mostly blue sky, puffy clouds dotting it here and there. "Not that I mind. The sun feels so good on my skin."

"It was a long winter." I stretched out my pale arms. Since our outing to the ice cream place in early March, winter had roared back to life, but as we started to close out the month, I hoped for more sunny days. I even wore cargo shorts today, which only caused Sarah to do her *I'm so disappointed in you* head shake.

"Fairy!" Fred hunched down to get a good look at the figurine, slanting his head in his usual way when studying something. He was so unlike his twin, who I doubted had spied any fairies at all on her quest for world domination. Probably a good thing since she was armed with a whacking stick. I wasn't certain how resilient the fairy statues were to such abuse.

"Did you read about the latest Forbes list of the world's richest people?" Willow gladly retook Freddie's hand, beaming at him, which he returned.

"Not yet. I bookmarked a few news articles I need to catch up on. What was the gist?"

"The richest people made a killing in 2020. There are six-hundred and sixty more billionaires than a year ago. And, there are four hundred and ninety-three new names on the list."

I whistled, which Fred mimicked. His effort resulted mostly in spit, not that it dimmed his happiness. Soon, he started to make bird-chirping sounds.

Willow continued, "Eighty-six percent of them are richer than they were before the pandemic."

Given what I'd been reading over the past twelve months, I wasn't surprised by the news, although it still made me sick to my stomach hearing the actual numbers.

"On the flip side," Willow said, "the number living in extreme poverty grew by one hundred and fifty million people."

I knew where this was heading, so I jumped in. "How does that compare to the income gap during the Gilded Age?"

"It's harder to affix numbers to it since the modern income tax hadn't been instituted, but it's estimated that in the final years of the 1800s, the wealthiest four thousand families in America, which was less than one percent of the entire population, had as much wealth as more than eleven million families combined. Fast forward to now, and it's estimated that the worth of just three of the wealthiest individuals in America equaled that of the bottom half of the population."

"P-pop-lation," Fred mimicked, filling me with immense pride at his budding genius. A second later, he shot up ahead to see what Ollie was poking at with her stick.

"It's not a worm, is it?" I shouted through my mask to Sarah.

She shook her head. "Rock."

"That's a relief," I said to Willow. "After I found Ollie torturing a worm in our backyard, I did some research, and they're capable of feeling pain. I can't abide anyone, let alone one of my children, causing another creature pain."

"I've never thought much about the pain tolerance of worms."

Perhaps as a way to change the topic, Willow pointed to a cardinal on a tree branch. I experienced a burst of adrenaline, but the little guy flittered away before I could get my hand into my shorts pocket.

"It's like they've all signed a pact to ensure I never get a photo," I complained.

"It's not from a lack of trying on your part." It was possible Willow did not strictly mean to praise my stick-to-itiveness with this observation, but I decided to take it that way.

"My goal before the fall semester arrives is to get a halfway decent shot," I declared. "Not a red blur."

As we continued to walk, we passed Maddie, who now stood over Ollie, keeping a vigilant eye on the stick whacking, along with Sarah angling herself to keep Fred, and Demi out of

Ollie's range. They had stopped next to a puddle, Fred and Demi each sticking little twigs into the surrounding mud as if conducting a science experiment while Ollie pounded away. A cringe zipped through me. My dislike of dirt, especially when muddy, would forever deny me the joys of having a lovely garden.

"Do you need help?" I asked Sarah, motioning to the kids but staying a good three feet from the yuck.

"Oh no. I know your thoughts on mud. I can handle it." Sarah motioned for Willow and me to continue along the path.

Rose and Troy, who was now carrying Calvin, were about a hundred feet ahead of us. Even though today's outing wasn't a race, I couldn't curb my instinct to quicken my pace, which Willow easily matched.

"What do you think we should call our newsletter?" I posed to Willow, knowing this was the reason she had brought up the latest billionaire numbers before my brain got sidetracked by the red cardinal, worms, and mud. "One of the articles I'd bookmarked for later, mentioned how the former president's ranking on the list had tumbled, as if that was the most important piece of news about billionaires, not the ever-growing divide between the haves and have-nots."

"Gotta love the mainstream news and their continual chase of clickbait while they ignore the chilling facts," Willow commented with more than a little disdain. "It's simply not right that a select few reap all the rewards while they work the poor to death. I'm worried about violence. A lot of it. Society simply can't keep rewarding the super-rich and ignoring everyone else."

A chill crept into the pit of my stomach as I added one more worry to the long list that would no doubt keep me up tonight. "The continual focus on the former guy is sickening, when it comes to this subject, or any subject, really. I don't deny the dude still has a lot to answer for. But the headline of the article, making it all about him and his wealth or lack of it, does highlight your case that more on-the-point news sources are needed. We can't be the only people on the planet who want to learn about the important matters and not the sensationalism of being a Kardashian, a Trump, or a three-legged alien."

Willow laughed at my lame attempt at a joke as if it were truly funny, something I was starting to appreciate about her. She simply had a good heart and never minded me being me. It was a relief since I'd pretty much determined I was never going to be anyone else.

"One of the Kardashians was kicked off the Forbes list for lying, but another went on in their place, so…" Willow joggled both hands up and down in the air as if to say the universe had remained in balance as far as the relative status of the Kardashians was concerned. "When should we really start to strategize this podcast of ours? I think you're on the right path. We need a name and soon."

"I'm free tonight." It was Saturday, but over the last twelve months of the pandemic, every day had blended into one, so I struggled to differentiate between work days and the weekend.

Apparently, Willow was having similar issues, which may have been because she didn't have a job, making every day the same. In any event, the moment she met my eyes, a smile spread across her face. "This is going to be so much fun!"

I nodded eagerly, aware that it was for the best the rest of our crew was too busy digging in the dirt to have heard this exchange. I doubted a single one of them would've agreed.

CHAPTER TWELVE

Later that night, Willow burst into the library, squealing, "We got our first sponsor!"

"For?" I set *The Way I See It* by Temple Grandin aside on my desk—more research on the A-word, although I wouldn't have been quick to admit it if asked—placing the pen I'd been using to mark up the margins on top of the book.

"For our enterprise!" She spun around three times on her tippy-toes.

"How is that possible? We haven't even started, meaning it hasn't been road-tested. Why would anyone sock money into something that hasn't proven itself?" While I liked the idea of having a sponsor, because that sounded fancy and something to add to my life accomplishment list in my perpetual competition to be the best Petrie, reality had taught me there was always a catch. Someone always wanted a payoff where money was concerned, and I was sure sponsorships were no different. "What do they get out of it?"

Willow took a deep breath and sat down in what I secretly called the *visitor's chair*, though I could never say this when

Sarah was around. "I just got off the phone with JJ, and the newsletter came up. She offered to sponsor it and the podcast."

"Wow! That's amazing." That put my mind at ease. Over the years, I'd come to trust JJ and had an excellent working relationship with her. She wasn't the type to fleece a friend.

"There's a hitch." Willow puffed out one cheek and then the other before slowly releasing it.

Uh-oh.

"Isn't there always?" I wasn't sure I really wanted to know the quid pro quo because JJ was one of the few people who gave me hope about humanity. I braced for the worst but really couldn't conjure up what that would be considering we were discussing a newsletter and podcast. "Hit me with it."

"We have to include the MDD brand in the title."

"Ah, I should have seen that coming. So, will this be an offshoot of *Matthews Daily Dish?*"

"Basically."

"What part of the name has to be used? The initials?"

"She wasn't particular about that, but given the *Dish* part represents her, and she's the one green-lighting the project, I'm leaning toward cramming *Dish* in somehow."

"Good because tossing in *Daily* isn't an option since it's weekly." I felt my cheeks turning red. "Sorry. Sometimes I have to say things out loud for them to make sense." I rubbed my chin, deep in thought. "Nothing's coming to mind. I've never been good in brainstorming sessions because my brain likes to marinate for at least seventy-two hours to find a solution, and it usually happens when I'm in the shower."

Willow's eyes widened. "Are you inviting me into the shower?"

"What? No!" I put a *stop right there* hand in the air, but this only made her laugh.

"I was kidding. I promise." Willow placed a hand on the Ralph Lauren pony embroidered on her pink shirt.

"That's a relief. Even though Sarah is used to me getting myself into pickles, that one would be particularly hard to explain." I wiggled in my seat, wanting to expunge the idea completely from my mind and body.

Willow's face lit up. "Okay, hear me out before you say no."

"Not a great start." I really hoped she wasn't back on the showering together thing.

She shushed me with a zip-it hand motion. "In a crowded market, we need a title that grabs someone's attention instantly, making them curious enough to click."

"Yes, it's called clickbait. JJ uses the word a lot and is always saying how it makes her cringe, although that doesn't stop her from seeking clicks. Her website depends on it."

"What if we blend all of our names together?" Willow clasped her hands in obvious delight.

"Willow Lizzie Dish. Lizzie Willow Dish. Or maybe you were thinking Dish Willow Lizzie?" The further I got with sounding out the possibilities, the more I faltered, not seeing why Willow was so excited by any of the prospects. "It doesn't flow off the tongue and does nothing to grab attention unless you're going for the boring crowd."

"There won't be anything boring about our venture. History is never boring." She winked at me, and considering we'd discussed ad nauseam how so many neophytes think it is, I knew she was joking. "How about: The Greene Petrie Dish." She made a *ta-da* motion with her hand.

I gaped at her, unable to move, let alone speak.

"I know I'd click on it to find out what the heck it meant," she said.

"But it makes it sound like some weird science project gone awry, not a history subject."

"Considering our take on history, that's not too far off the mark."

"What do you mean?" I swiped up the pen to write the

name on a Post-it Note, needing to see it in print. Frankly, it didn't help me warm up to the idea.

"We'll be breaking down income inequality, which is like a social experiment gone off course. Furthermore, history has gone astray on more occasions than I can remember. Human interactions have been messy since the cave people days."

"Okay, but what if we lop off the Petrie part? I've never liked my last name, especially after Peter's arrest." I tapped the pen against my thigh.

"No one really remembers that now."

The hubbub had died down, what with COVID and a million other scandals that had happened since his trial. "That's true, but I do. Along with all the times I got spit on." I cringed. "The name doesn't have the best connotations for me."

"We have to include you. I wouldn't feel right not doing so. Besides, it's your name that adds the pizzazz. We need it!" She clicked her fingers.

I grimaced as I imagined a Petri dish overflowing with green slime.

"I know your thoughts about your last name, but consider this. You've built a reputation in academic circles and on JJ's show."

"Yes, but I have everyone call me Lizzie for a reason. I never go by Dr. Petrie. Not even my students call me that." I squirmed yet again, and it occurred to me that maybe it was working my abs. If so, I should keep it up. My bulge needed some reining in, but with the kids and research, finding time for workouts was getting harder and harder.

"Maybe it's time you reclaim your name and shape it into something that makes you proud." From her broad smile, Willow seemed sold on the idea.

"Can we continue to mull it over?" By that, I meant I needed time to come up with a way to get her to see how it was a terrible idea. Horrendous. Maybe it was time to go for a long walk and then take an extra-long shower to come up with the perfect name to get her off the worst possible name train.

"I'm not sure you'll be able to sway me from the title, no matter how hard you try. I'm going to workshop it!" With that, she hopped up from the visitor's chair and beelined for the exit.

"I guess that's it for today's meeting," I said to my book since no one else was in the room. Well, there was Hank sleeping on the corner of my desk, but our cat didn't give me a thought unless it was time to be fed, so he didn't bother lifting his head. In fact, he buried it deeper into his front legs as if saying, "Be quiet, human slave. Can't you tell I'm sleeping?"

"You're just like the rest of the family." I shook my pen at him. "What did Willow mean she was going to workshop it? Does that mean there's hope yet?"

"Talking to ghosts?" Sarah slinked around the door of the office wearing her *gotcha* smile and holding a glass of her end-of-day mommy juice. "Is this part of your nighttime routine?"

"I was talking to our cat."

"You'd have better luck summoning a ghost if you want someone to listen." Sarah scratched behind one of Hank's ears, which he allowed for one second before taking a swipe at her hand.

"Tell me about it."

"Have you made your decision about the twins and school?"

The topic came out of nowhere, instantly sending me hunching in my chair. "It's still early. We don't even know if school will be in-person or not."

"Yes, but avoiding the topic simply won't do. The kids need school. That's not up for debate."

"I'm a professor. Naturally I agree with the importance of education. It worries me, though. I know the vast majority of students aren't getting sick, but that less than one percent chance stops my heart. Then there's Fred. What school would be best for him if our suspicions about him being on the spectrum are correct?"

"I've been doing some research on that." Sarah shifted on the couch, placing one foot under her. "I know how adamantly you've been against public school, but many parents say it's the best place for kids on the spectrum."

"Why?" My hackles were up before I realized it, and the question came out with a snap. "Is it because they think autistic kids are dumb and don't deserve a proper education?"

"Whoa. Down girl." Sarah held up a hand. "It's the opposite. They're required by law to have resources for kids with certain needs. One of the moms I've chatted with, who has a kid in private school, had to have her child evaluated through the public school, and all their services came through there, too."

"You mean, they were paying all that money for nothing?" The look of triumph in Sarah's eyes told me I'd gone exactly where she'd intended for me to. I hated wasting money.

"By every measure, the public schools in our district are pretty fantastic," Sarah added, which I already knew since the real estate agent had gone on and on about it when we'd been house hunting. "I'm leaning toward that option, which also extends our deadline to decide if we enroll them because no matter what, a child has the right to go to public school."

"I like that—more time to think." I relaxed into my chair, feeling a weight had been lifted off my shoulders.

"I thought you might."

"Speaking of mulling things over, what are your thoughts on the name: The Greene Petrie Dish?"

Sarah tipped her head back and laughed. "What's this about?"

"That's what Willow wants to call our newsletter and podcast. Oh!" I perked up in my seat. "We got our first sponsor!"

"I leave you alone for a couple of hours so you can get some work done, and the next thing I know, you and Willow are starting a media empire."

"I can't tell if you're teasing."

"I know." Sarah's eyes twinkled merrily. "I love the way you tilt your head when utterly flummoxed."

"You still haven't said what you think of the name."

"It would catch my interest. That's for sure."

"Damn it." I tossed my pen onto the desk, causing Hank to bolt. "I'm sorry, Hank!"

He disappeared out the door, a swish of his tail letting me know there was no forgiveness on the horizon.

"I don't think he'll listen to your podcast, if that makes a difference," Sarah offered by way of cheering me up.

"Back to the name. You'd really click on something that sounds so revolting?"

"Yes. Isn't that what you want?" Sarah shifted on the sofa and took a sip of her wine.

"But it's not for the reason I want." I flicked a hand in the air. "It's a cheap way to get attention."

"That's the way of the world now." Sarah set her glass on the end table. "If that's the name you go with, think of it this way. If people do follow it, you're still getting your ideas out there. Isn't that more important than why they click?"

"The ends justify the means? Is that what you're saying?"

"Yeah. I guess it is."

"That's very Machiavellian of you," I pointed out, somewhat impressed. "Do you know how he was tortured? They tied his arms behind his back, tossed a rope over a beam, pulled him up, and then dropped him."

"Why are you sharing that detail with me when I'm trying to unwind on a Saturday night?" She rested her head on the back of the couch with a sigh.

"Because I learned it when studying *The Prince*, and now,

whenever I hear or think of him, that vision plays in my head." I shrugged. "I don't understand how my brain works. I just go with it."

"Clearly." She swept up her wineglass and took a healthy swig. "Can we talk about something else?"

"The topics I'm focusing on at the moment are income inequality, the rise of white supremacy, autism, and the threat to the planet." I tapped the stack of books next to me, one on each of the aforementioned subjects. "Take your pick, but Medieval torture methods might be more palatable considering how the rest of my list is impacting our present-day lives."

"What if we did something other than talk?"

I stroked my chin as I ran through the possibilities. "I've been meaning to watch the Ken Burns documentary on the Roosevelt family."

"Seriously, Lizzie." Sarah propped up her chin with a palm. "I came in here to seduce you."

"Then why did you start out by ambushing me on the school topic?"

"Foreplay?" Sarah arched her brows, wiggling them suggestively.

"Interesting technique. Why did you sit on the couch when I'm all the way over here?"

She met my eyes. "To fuck with you, obviously."

"It's working." I circled a finger around my temple. "Completely baffled and even though you said you want to seduce me, I can't help but ponder if you're saying that to get my hopes up, only to smash them to pieces."

"Do you really think I'd do that?" Sarah studied me with a look that was more puzzled than hurt.

"Not really, but it's been a pattern in my life. Being the butt of jokes and cruel tricks. I've been making a list of all the times it's happened."

Sarah gave me a sympathetic head bob. "Kids can be cruel."

"I wasn't talking about kids. My list centers on things Peter and Mom did, but now that you mention it…" I clicked my pen and made a note to start a list of bullies from my school days. "This is going to be quite the project."

"Honey, I'm not like any of your tormenters. You do know that, right?"

"I know. It's just—" I flicked the pages of the Temple Grandin book. "Reading about others who are autistic is drudging up lots of uncomfortable memories."

"Do you want to talk about that?"

"Yes, but not right now." I touched my tongue to my lips, fixing her with a hopeful look. "I believe you mentioned something else guaranteed to take my mind off bullies, income inequality, and the end of the world."

Sarah's mouth formed a sly smile. "As a matter of fact, I did."

"I'd like to know more about this miracle cure."

She beckoned me with a crooked finger. "Come over here, and find out all about it."

CHAPTER THIRTEEN

WHILE THE EXPRESSION on her face was sexy as hell, my brain—in evil cooperation with my mouth—decided to launch a torpedo into the prospect of something delightful. Naturally, because that was the story of my life.

"Did you come in here to demand sex," I asked with a level of suspicion befitting a television detective.

"Does it matter?" Sarah asked, pointing out the obvious. She gave me her crooked smile that exclaimed two things: you're an idiot, and I absolutely adore this side of you.

"I'd like to know. That's all." For the love of God, why? How many morons had a gorgeous wife who liked to get freaky in the sheets?

"The things that trip you up make me laugh. They really do."

"Are you laughing with me or at me?" I demanded, persisting in my quest to keep from getting lucky with a tenaciousness that surprised even me.

"Is it possible to be doing both?"

This short-circuited my brain. I knew two things could be simultaneously true, but in this particular instance, did I want them to be? So many people had laughed at me in my life. I didn't want Sarah to fall into that category.

Perhaps she sensed this because she clarified, "With you, Lizzie. Always *with* you. Now, are you done being your own worst enemy?"

"I haven't decided." I crossed my arms, pretending to still be mad, but my mood was suddenly playful. Her answer had reassured me.

"Since when are you not in the mood?" She arched an eyebrow, which was very unfair because if I hadn't been in the mood before, I certainly was now. Even so, I felt compelled to drag this game out a teensy bit more.

"To be honest, I'm having a hard time getting The Green Petrie Dish out of my head." That much was true, and to drive that point home, I experienced a full body quiver. "There are some things in life I'll never figure out. One: why you like me. Two: what people want from me. Three: everything in between."

"So, basically, life."

"Exactly. It's exhausting always trying to do mental calculations to figure out people's motives."

"When it comes to me, right now, I have one motive." Sarah got to her feet, walked to me, and plopped herself down on my lap, her knees holding me captive. There was no need to ask her what that one motive was.

"You're so much more flexible than I am." I craned my neck to get the full picture. "With a very nice ass."

"That's always nice to hear, and this is how I want to say thank you." She kissed the side of my neck.

This time, the shiver working through me was oh, so delightful. "I like how you do that."

Instead of asking what, like I would have done, Sarah continued up toward my lobe, nibbling on it, causing me to squirm underneath her, fighting the urge to pull away since it was almost too much pleasure at once.

"What's the matter, sweetheart?" she asked with a mischievous look. Not waiting for me to answer, she followed up the question by dipping her tongue into my ear, one of my major weaknesses.

"Nn-nothing. Keep… dd-doing… th-that." My breath hitched as my body ignited. It was nearly impossible to get any words out.

"Are you sure?" Sarah switched to my other ear. "It seems to be doing something to you. Can you handle it?"

"I don't rightly know," I admitted with a nervous chuckle, "but I'm game to see if this is how I leave the world."

She laughed, rolling those lovely deep-brown eyes. "Are you going to take me upstairs now?"

"We basically have the house to ourselves, aside from Maddie and Willow. Do we always have to hide in the bedroom?"

"Yes because even though I'm still flexible, I'm also nearing forty."

"I think you have a few years before the middle age milestone." I tried to remember her exact age but failed. Numbers always eluded me, and I wasn't quick enough to subtract the current year with her birth one. "How many is it?"

"A hundred, at least." Sarah pressed a finger to my lips. "Stop mentioning it. I can reference me being almost forty. You can't. Not ever."

"Got it." I motioned for her to get up. "Come on, my young chickadee. Let's go upstairs and not make babies." I pinched one eye shut, going over that sentence. "Pretty sure I need to workshop that come-on line some more."

"You think?" Sarah stood, putting out a hand to help me off the chair. "Come on, old lady."

"Why can you say that, but I can't say you're almost forty? I don't get your rules." I puffed out my bottom lip, pouting, but damn, her way of looking at me with those soulful eyes was making it hard to concentrate on anything.

"I'm not asking you to understand my rules, just to follow them."

"You're such a dictator!"

"You would know, my darling Hitler expert."

I could have said a lot more on the subject, but for once I didn't take the bait, perhaps because Sarah had hefted her shirt up, showing me the girls—or the two swells above the bra, anyway, which were so damn intoxicating on their own I didn't need to see more. At least, not right away.

"Now, you're really cheating." I took her hand and led her out of the library, up the stairs, and into our bedroom.

"Time for me to show you who's really in charge," Sarah teased after the door clicked shut.

I stood rooted to my spot, suddenly overtaken by a nervousness, which was so intense I wasn't sure I'd ever experienced anything like it before. Maybe the first day of kindergarten or being called on to speak in public without warning. I was frozen in place.

Sarah quirked an eyebrow as if trying to figure out if this was part of an act or if there was something truly wrong. "Lizzie? What's the matter?"

"Is there something wrong with me? Even after all of these years of us being together, I get nervous," I confessed but forced myself to keep my eyes on her lovely chocolate browns, which always had a way of soothing me.

"Yeah, I've noticed. FYI, I find it endearing. It does make me wonder why, though."

"Because you're stunning." I mimed curvaceous with my hands. "Not just that way, either. You're stunning in every way, and I'm not at all, no matter the category."

Sarah slanted her head. "I strongly disagree."

Nervous laughter escaped me.

She inched toward me, slowly, almost as if she didn't want to spook me even more than I already was. "You have the most amazing blue eyes. So dark I feel like you can see deep inside me."

"I feel the same when you look at me, but I'm afraid of what you'll uncover. You have no idea how scared I am all the time. Of losing you. The kids. Like I'm waiting for the day when everyone finally sees I'm a fraud. I'm not a brilliant historian, or a loving wife, or a devoted mother." I tapped a finger to my head. "Up here, I'm always terrified every second of every single day."

"I know, sweetheart, but none of the things you've listed is true. It'll never happen." She was one step away from me. "No matter what, I'll always be by your side."

"Even if I start cohosting a podcast named The Greene Petrie Dish?" I shook like I'd swallowed a live worm, something I would never do, by the way.

"You may not like the name, but the fact that you're even contemplating this project proves to me how brave you truly are. It's one of the things I've always admired about you. Your courage in spite of your fear." Her lips were on mine, and all the worry whooshed out of my body, like it always did when she touched me.

I kicked up the heat of the kiss, my hand reaching behind her head, my fingers entangled in her hair, not wanting our connection ever to break. How did this magical creature love me with all her being when I was Lizzie the Lesbian who destroyed all? Like my mother used to say.

No, Lizzie.

Get out of your head.

I walked Sarah backward to the foot of the bed and stripped off her shirt, my chest heaving when I got a good, long look at her new lacy bra. "You never forget how much I love sexy lingerie."

"I love the way your eyes light up when you discover a new bra."

I cupped her breast over the satin. "It's the best kind of treasure. Well, aside from having you by my side." I reached for her hand, loving the way our wedding rings clinked together.

"In case you want to know one of your superpowers, you're doing it now. You're the sweetest and most sincere person I've ever known. Not everyone can be truly honest."

We kissed again. Slowly. Sensuously.

My hands worked around to unhook the bra, my mouth trailing down her left arm as I meticulously slid the strap down, repeating the actions on the other arm, working all the way to her fingertips and raising her hand to my lips.

Her nips came to life, and my lips wrapped around the shy one, wanting to rouse it further.

Sarah undid her jeans, and I stopped momentarily to help her step out of them before I shoved her onto her back on the bed, causing her to bounce up half an inch, laughing.

I hurriedly ditched my clothes and climbed on top of her. "Now, where was I?"

She looked longingly at her nipple.

"That's right. I feel a connection to this one since it's also the fearful type." I eased the nub into my mouth, mixing up the pressure of my bites, thrilled by its reaction. Not wanting to neglect the other, I stopped there before I started my trek down.

My tongue gorging on the tantalizing taste of her desire.

When I arrived where Sarah wanted me most, I eased a finger inside, and my tongue settled on her clit, causing Sarah to gasp in anticipation. It was the most amazing sound because it held the promise of our love, and I fucking adored this woman with every fiber of my being.

One of her hands cupped the back of my head, while her other hand reached for my free one, our fingers wrapping, entwined.

This was the definition of love, and for many blissful minutes, we were completely connected.

CHAPTER FOURTEEN

IT WAS two months nearly to the day from when Willow had proposed the podcast and newsletter idea, and if she had it her way, we would've been starting an entire media company on the first day we launched. Who knew the Pilates fiend was such a business shark?

Back to the matter at hand, I sat in the semi-finished portion of the basement. It had been retrofitted into a podcast studio, and we were seconds away from recording the inaugural episode.

Willow sat at the far end of the table, in front of a newly purchased microphone on a retractable arm. It looked like what they used in radio stations, or at least the ones I had seen in movies, and I had to admit I loved the setup because it screamed, "We're super professional!"

I had the same mic and arm sitting in front of me, and I adjusted it closer to my mouth, feeling the butterflies swarming in the pit of my stomach, ready to take their first swoop over the edge. Ever since I was a kid, before embarking on anything new, I'd always immediately had the urge to pee. Being an adult now, I tightened my legs and pressed on. Experience had taught me that as soon as I got going, that sensation would pass.

"Ready?" Willow asked, but her words filtered through my headphones, which made it seem even weirder but in a cool way, or *totally lit* as my students would say. At least, I think that was what it meant. I'd recently heard Maddie use the word Gucci for awesome, but I wasn't sure if she was fucking with me to see if I'd fall for it. That was something she'd do to me.

I nodded to Willow, indicating I was ready. Only then did it dawn on me this was an audio recording, which necessitated speaking. "Yep. Let's b-begin," I stuttered.

Admittedly, that wasn't the best start to my podcasting career, even if the record button hadn't been pressed yet. Too wimpy and formal for this medium, which I'd read was supposed to sound more like a conversation, not a lecture.

Willow gave me a thumbs-up, cleared her throat, and swallowed some water. "Welcome to the inaugural episode of The Green Petrie Dish."

"That's such a terrible name. Totally not Gucci," I interjected but then quickly covered my microphone, mouthing an apology for my outburst, which I'd sworn to myself I wouldn't do. Also, I'd let the dubious slang term I'd learned from Maddie fly, which I still wasn't certain about. Now, I was frantically looking it up on the Urban Dictionary website on my phone, but all I could find was a definition that said it referred to the area between the anus and balls.

What? That couldn't be right.

Feeling like the heartbeat in my throat was practically strangling me, I realized my error. I'd typed the word *Gooch*, not *Gucci*. Fortunately, when I tapped out the correct letters, I was able to confirm Maddie hadn't led me astray.

Willow stuck her thumb in the air, but then reversed it, the thumb pointing downward, with a questioning expression, and I interpreted that was her way of asking if everything was okay, or should we bail and start over. I circled my index fingers in the air to say keep rolling. Then I remembered for the second time in as many minutes that I was supposed to use words. Unless she'd meant for me to respond silently this time because she hadn't spoken either. I honestly had no idea. This was not going well.

"That's my podcasting partner, Lizzie Petrie, who hasn't been shy about hating the name of our show ever since I first proposed it. Oh, the battles we've had behind the scenes."

"Battles!" I made a *pffft* sound, whatever reluctance I'd had about speaking disappearing the moment I opened my mouth. "Please. Once the name entered your mind, you were sold. No matter how hard I tried to convince you otherwise. I would like to assure the listeners that despite the terrible name, I promise you the content will be great. Or should I say totally Gucci? I'm not sure I'm using the word correctly, but I can tell you I don't recommend shortening it to Gooch. Did you know that's the area between the anus and balls? Not only am I almost forty, meaning I have one foot in the grave for all the Gen Z listeners, but I'm a lesbian, so Gooch does nothing for me. Anyway, I'd like to reiterate, while the podcast name is hideous, the content will be superb."

Oh, God. Had I taken a single breath during all that? I was burning up. It had to be two-hundred and fifty degrees in the basement. I pulled my T-shirt collar away from my neck and guzzled some ice water.

Willow, who had been laughing during my rambling, lit up by the end of my statement. "By jove, I think you've come up with our tagline: terrible name, great content."

"It does have a nice sound to it." I stared at the microphone, repeating the phrase over and over in my head, liking it more each time. "Yeah. Terrible name, great content. That's us."

"You see, folks, this is why I wanted Lizzie—don't ever say her last name, by the way—as the cohost. She's honest and never holds back. A key ingredient for a podcast partner. Besides, she drops in interesting nuggets like Gooch."

"Oh, no. Don't say nuggets and Gooch together." I waved my hands in the air, even though the audience wouldn't see that. "My outbursts might be because I'm autistic. Well, that's kinda self-diagnosed because my doctor didn't give a shit when I tried talking about it at my appointment. I'd only recently stumbled on some research about autism in girls, and the more I read, the more I saw so many similarities to myself. Honestly, all of them but when I tried talking to my doctor, she kept telling me to drink water. Not simply for my autism, but for everything, including my allergies and dry skin. I think she should go into medicine for camels, not humans."

Willow looked up from the microphone but rolled with the punches. "That's something I didn't know about you until now."

My brow wrinkled as I tried to puzzle out which thing she hadn't known. "The water?"

"No, the other part," Willow said. "About you being autistic."

I stiffened, worried where she was going with this. "If you'd known, would you still have asked me to do this podcast?"

"Abso-frigging-lutely!"

Instantly, I felt lighter and more relaxed. "Aw, that's kind of you to say and with such enthusiasm. Listeners, let's see how she feels by the end of this episode, or better yet, if we hit episode one hundred. That's some serious hard time with the likes of me. Ask my wife, who luckily isn't in the room because I think she'd be cringing right about now. Hearing me say Gooch would probably have broken her."

"One hundred episodes. That sounds like a dare!" Willow laughed. "I accept. Now for today's question: Can you guess the time period for the following? One: an increase of white supremacy groups to take back control via brutality and scare tactics. Two: demands to stop immigrants from overwhelming our borders. Three: linking the rights of labor with racism, by shouting we're at war with Latinos, Asians, and labor unions. Four: enduring one of the greatest economic downturns, while simultaneously claiming communism will kneecap capitalism. Five: Americans killing their fellow Americans at record numbers. Six: the fear that the next inauguration will fail to usher in the newly elected president."

As Willow took a breath, I said, "We'll give you a second to digest all of that and vote for what year we're describing. It's too bad we can't take a live poll."

"It is," Willow agreed, "but should we put the listeners out of their misery and let them in on the answer?"

We'd practiced this part, so I knew it was my job to say, "While many of the conditions Willow listed sound a lot like the twelve months we've just barely survived, we are, in fact, outlining one of the pivotal years in the history of the United States of America. Can I get a drum roll?" This hadn't been part of our rehearsal, but Willow didn't miss a beat, banging on the desk for me. "The answer is 1877."

"1877 was during the Gilded Age, which is my area of expertise. Now, Lizzie, your focus is early twentieth century history, which covers the 1900s 'til the end of World War II."

"Correct."

"Would you have guessed the right year?"

"It depends. If everything was listed while I was currently studying that time period, which I did during my undergrad days, I would have, naturally. But, if we were at a bar today, chatting, and you put me on the spot and asked me the year, heck no. I have to admit, as a historian, I would have been completely humiliated."

"That would be an off-the-wall question to ask, unless we were playing pub trivia."

"I think that might actually be a game I'd like. There aren't many." I took a breath, looking back at my script. "We should mention, while early twentieth century history is my jam, I focused more on the European front, the rise of the Nazis and fascism in particular. Since embarking on this project with you, I've come to learn 1877 is one of the pivotal years when the US almost tore apart again so soon after the Civil War. In my humble opinion, I don't think 1877 gets enough attention." I was really warming to the topic now and launched in headfirst. "Pundits on television keep referencing the Civil War but not 1877. It was a critical time because former slaves had been granted the right to vote, but the elites in the South didn't want them to, fearing they'd lose their power. It's so unnervingly similar to the Republican Party playbook since the Reagan era when he declared in his inaugural address *government wasn't the solution to our problem; government is the problem*. Most of my life, Republican leaders have tried to take away rights of those they're scared of, or in my case since I'm a lesbian, denying me basic rights most people take for granted. When I first realized I was gay, I never thought I'd be able to legally marry."

At this point, I gasped for air, which is when I realized I'd been talking nonstop for who knew how long. I wondered if we'd have to record that bit again. I'd monopolized the conversation and spoken a mile a minute.

"It's crazy to think about," Willow said, jumping into the opening I'd left and not sounding annoyed by how I'd rambled on. "It also points to how America is on yet another precipice of destroying the country and the threat to our democratic institutions. While the conditions for what we're living through today are different, it's like certain forces are pulling moves from the 1877 playbook, which is why we thought this would be a great way to open our first podcast episode. We plan to take a deep dive into the good, the bad, and the ugly of The Gilded Age and to compare it to present day. While it may be depressing at times, Lizzie and I are oddly optimistic because the US survived 1877. Yes, we admit many of the major concerns from that time period haven't been addressed, and that's part of the underlying cause of all the unrest we're still witnessing. Things are different today, such as technological advances, but we fervently believe in understanding our past to learn from it and apply those lessons to the present."

"Oh gosh," I joked, "are you going to make me say the line every history professor utters on the first day of class?"

Willow laughed. "Go for it."

Those who fail to learn from history are doomed to repeat it."

"You have that delivery down!"

"It's possible I quote it not only to my students but to random people I bump into at the grocery store. Given how the major events in 1877 sound now, I have to say Churchill's line is apt. So, let's do our part. Learn from our past mistakes to make things better. Our children's futures depend on it, and as a mother of four, I'm committed to this goal. Let's make the world a better place while chatting about history because when you think about it, it's the greatest story ever told, and it has everything ranging from warfare to love."

"That's so true. We're asking you to join us. It may seem odd pairing our backgrounds, but we believe together we can help explain some things that are going on today, cutting through the bullshit to showcase the unvarnished annals of history. Now, we should get this out of the way right out of the gate. We're both historians, so expect a lot of bickering. That's what historians do, but it's how we get to the bottom of things."

"It might not be pretty, much like the title of this show, but it won't be stuffy. We promise that."

Willow, who had the announcer voice down, brought us out of the episode, and before I knew it, we were done.

"How'd that feel?" she asked, clicking some buttons on her laptop.

"I give myself a C minus," I replied as all the mistakes I'd made paraded through my mind. It was so much different than giving a lecture or even JJ's show, where I usually answered questions and argued with other guests to score points, but in a professional way. I was the type that necessitated structure and competition. Willow wasn't the type I wanted to screech at to prove her wrong. From the research I'd done, the podcast format rebelled against the rules of verbal jousting I understood and thrived on.

"Don't be that way. It was a fantastic start. I can't wait to hear the final product." With that, she took off her headphones and left the room.

I sat in my chair, staring at the microphone, wondering if this podcast thing was really such a good fit for someone like me. Who knew what shit would fly out of my mouth when in such an informal setting? One episode in, and I'd already dropped the word Gooch, not to mention the A-bomb. Why had I brought that up? Aside from Sarah and my doctor, I hadn't told a soul about my suspicion that I was autistic. Now Willow knew, but at least that was where it would end, other than a few strangers who might stumble on the podcast, and I would never meet them in real life anyway.

CHAPTER FIFTEEN

By the time the first podcast episode was released the following week, I'd blocked it out for the most part. That was one of the perks of working so much. My brain couldn't spin out on one impending date on the calendar. Aside from random thoughts about general performance while recording the episode, it wasn't until Willow took a seat at dinner on our launch date that I came to understand I had a problem.

"We've had over two thousand listens." Willow announced as she placed a slice of Hawaiian pizza on her plate.

"Already?" I held a pizza slice to my mouth, trying to prevent a piece of sausage from falling off. "Wow. I guess I didn't factor in that people would actually listen."

Willow laughed in her carefree way. "Let's hope they do!"

Frankly, I was hoping the opposite. Two thousand people in a few hours? What had I gotten myself into?

Sarah smothered my knee with a hand under the table, giving it a squeeze. "I'm proud of you two."

"Have you listened?" I asked, while chanting in my head, *why would anyone ever listen to me, an idiot?*

She nodded.

I gulped a bite of pizza, practically swallowing it whole. After forcing the lump down my throat with water, I said, "I'm not sure I really thought this out."

Maddie was about to say something, but Sarah jumped in first. "Don't overthink it. One of the great things about podcasts is they're not always scripted. Sure, you had notes typed out, but they're more like guidelines, and people want a more natural conversation that takes twists and turns."

"Yes, but I think one of the twists was I diagnosed myself with… you know."

"You did." Her expression blared with pride, confusing me even more.

"Isn't that arrogant, though? I mean, I haven't been officially diagnosed, although I've read everything I can get my hands on, and it's hard to deny all the ticks in the spectrum column." I made a check mark in the air.

"Your experience with your doctor is also an example of how women are ignored by the medical community," Sarah pointed out. "It fits the topic of your podcast in a roundabout way. How for eons, history has been dominated by those in power doing all they can to keep the masses down in every way possible, including not listening to women when they have medical needs."

I took another bite of pizza, chewing it more carefully this time to avoid choking. "It's weird, though. I know I lecture, appear on TV shows, write books, and I've been a guest on other podcasts, but being a guest is easier. Cohosting puts the onus on me to be entertaining, edgy, or whatever to keep people tuned in. Not to mention, it's still difficult to comprehend that people actually read or listen to what I have to say. I'm not comfortable with that."

"I know, Lizzie, but I think you're about to find out how many people listen and read your books." Sarah gave me a supportive smile.

"B-bbut that's terrifying!" I smothered my mouth with my palm and sucked in a breath before speaking through the cracks of my fingers. "I'm an idiot," I said, unable to keep the words locked inside my head.

"No." Sarah's tone was almost scolding. "Don't say or even think that. You see the world in a very unique way. There's nothing wrong with that. Sometimes, it even provides some humor. I think listeners will appreciate that aspect about you, like I do."

Willow met Maddie's gaze briefly before saying, "It was an extremely natural and honest conversation. However, if you want me to take it down, I will."

I contemplated that as I swallowed another bite of pizza. "No, leave it. I need to pretend no one will listen so I can stay natural." I swiveled my head to Sarah. "If you do listen in the future, can you not tell me you did? I'm pretty sure with enough mental gymnastics, I can pretend I'm talking to Willow and no one else."

"Listen? Listen to what?" Sarah gave me a smile that sealed the deal.

"You're the best."

"Speaking of the podcast that shall never be discussed," Maddie began with a booming voice. Now that she was finally wading into the conversation, I detected Willow and Sarah holding their breath. While I'd mentioned my suspicion about being autistic on the episode, I hadn't discussed it with Maddie, who was notorious for teasing me, and I'd been avoiding her as much as possible despite living under the same roof. "Can you two discuss the people who've been ignored for centuries? It's like women, people of color, children, and so many others never existed until very recently. I'm sure there are plenty of badass bitches to dish about. I'd love hearing about them, not political leaders. I'm sick of politics."

"Badass Bitches." Willow snapped her fingers. "Damn, that would have been a great name for the podcast."

"Can we change it to that?" Hope flooded through me. "It's way better than what we have."

"Sorry. The Green Petrie Dish is getting a lot of play on social media. It's doing the heavy lifting, which is it's job."

I gnashed my teeth at Willow.

She offered a sweet smile in return.

Maddie got up from the table. "Anyone need a refill?"

I looked questioningly at Sarah, baffled that Maddie hadn't said a word about the other thing. I'd been certain she would tease me mercilessly over the A-word.

Sarah gave me a knowing smile, and I wondered if she had pulled Maddie aside and threatened to knock her lights out if Maddie said anything negative about my confession. While I didn't condone violence, the thought of Sarah going to bat for me made me feel oddly protected and loved.

CHAPTER SIXTEEN

THE FOLLOWING EVENING, Maddie entered my office, and I had no doubt she wanted to corner me to discuss the subject of the A-word revelation. She stood awkwardly in the doorway, her eyes downcast, wringing her fingers. It was the look I imagined children got when they had to turn themselves in to the police for stealing a pack of gum.

So far, I'd never had to deal with this situation with my own children. This wasn't necessarily because they had no larcenous tendencies, but they were too young to venture into stores on their own, and they hadn't stepped foot in one during COVID, anyway. Realistically, Olivia was my bet for the most likely to become a thief. I could picture her grinning ear to ear if she swiped anything.

Maddie finally inched inside, taking a seat on the couch. I stayed behind my desk, needing the extra barrier. I wondered if she needed the same.

"I've been reading a book that I thought you'd find interesting," she started out, still unable to meet my eyes.

I held my breath, waiting for the punchline.

"It's about a woman like... you."

"A history professor?" My joke came out a little stiffer than I'd intended. I really didn't want to discuss this with anyone, least of all Maddie, which only made my podcast confession all the more intriguing. If I didn't want to talk about it, why in the hell did I blurt it out and then tell Willow to keep the episode up after learning it was actually being listened to? I'd been offered an easy way out, yet I hadn't taken it.

Meanwhile, Maddie may not have realized I'd been teasing because she looked ready to sink into the floor. "No. Not similar in that way."

"A mother?" Okay, I should have let her off the hook at this point, but did I mention I didn't want to talk about it?

"Yes, she's a mom, but that wasn't what I meant, either."

It was odd to see Maddie struggle to find the right words, and I had to admit I was kinda enjoying the moment, even if I wished we weren't going down this road together. It was childish, but can you blame me? I'd been the butt of her jokes on so many occasions, and now she was the one squirming on the end of the hook. Finally, I relented. "I know what you came here to discuss. The A-word."

Maddie nodded, a look of relief passing over her features not unlike the one that comes from making it home just in time when you really have to pee. "I also watched some YouTube videos about autis—the A-word, that is."

I started laughing. "How did any of us ever figure shit out before YouTube?"

Maddie laughed with me, but then her expression turned serious. "Have you mentioned this to your dad or brother?"

I shook my head. "Uh, I hadn't even considered it."

"I know when you were diagnosed with Graves' Disease you didn't tell them, but maybe they'd want to know about this. It's your choice, but if it was my sister or daughter, I'd like to know."

"It hasn't been such a secret in my family that I'm different.

Not solely because I'm gay. There has always been something else about me, and I'm just starting to get my feet under the reason. It's hard to give voice to it." Let alone understand the fifty different messages blaring through my brain every second of the day.

"I'm so sorry you're going through this." Maddie sighed, her expression sincere. "I know your family wasn't the best during your childhood, although things were starting to get better. With COVID, though, it's hard again because you haven't been able to see them in real life. Chatting on Zoom isn't the same. It's nearly impossible to have a heart-to-heart."

"I'm sick and tired of Zoom." I held a pen between my forefingers, wiggling it back and forth as I channeled some of the nervous energy this conversation was creating. "I'll give telling my family some thought."

"You've already told everyone else, in a roundabout way," Maddie pointed out.

"I… I didn't mean to say anything about it on the podcast. It just came out. It seems I'm having a harder time keeping things in these days, and I don't understand my motivations. Like I don't want to hide anymore, but I do on some level. I don't know if I am, well, you know or not, but I'm not like everyone else. My research… I'm learning that's okay. I need to get to a place where thinking about it doesn't throw me off. Like when I came out of the closet. For the first few years, I couldn't banish the thought I had a Scarlet L carved into my forehead and that's all people would see when they met me. Now, it's like I'm etching a big fat A next to it."

"LA?" Maddie made an attempt at a goofy face. "Everyone loves LA."

I rolled my eyes, but it did make me smile.

"Believe it or not," Maddie said with a shrug, "I'm trying to be supportive."

"Oh, I know." I pressed my lips together to keep from laughing at her predicament. "It must be killing you."

She leaned back against the couch. "No, I wouldn't say that. Willow's been talking to me about how much I tease you, and she's helping me dig deep to find the cause. I think the biggest reason is things seem so easy for you, and I've always struggled."

"You think things are easy for me?" This time, there was no stopping it. I burst into laughter. "I've never seen my life that way."

"Maybe not, but from my perspective, you have a great career, a fantastic wife, and great kids. For so long, I've been on the cliff's edge. I can't shake the feeling that I won't be able to come back to safety, and I'll never have everything you do."

"You still feel this way?" I sat up straight in my chair, alarmed.

"Yes and no. Willow helps keep me centered, but I'm afraid. You, Sarah, and the kids have kept me from plunging." She made a motion with her hand and accompanied it with a sound effect resulting in a spectacular crash. "Willow wants us to get our own place, but I don't know how to survive without the family madness here. Whenever I am in this house, there's someone to distract me. I need that. The thoughts in my head scare me."

"I get that part and the fear of settling down, although for the opposite reason. When Sarah wanted us to settle down together, I didn't want the chaos. I wanted my own space. It took me a long time to come to terms with how much loving someone changes every aspect of your life. I almost lost Sarah because of my fear."

"I remember." Maddie looked down at her folded hands. "I'm worried I'll screw things up with Willow."

"Have you talked to her about these feelings?"

"Yeah. She's doing her best to understand. She wants us to

have more alone time, which I get, but I'm slammed with work, and if we do buy a place, it'll be up to me to pay the bills until Willow figures things out. Not that I'm rushing her. I want her to take the time to make the right decision. Still, it's a lot of pressure. Besides, I love living here, and one day, I might be able to rent an office space so I'm not working out of the bedroom. It's not like Willow doesn't like it here. I truly believe she does, and she loves the kids. Maybe it's simply the cramped bedroom. The majority of my clients want ways to carve out space for some quiet, so…" She completed the thought with a shrug.

I weighed her words, my brain circling back to Sarah not having a space and how I knew this should be rectified. But I needed to respond to Maddie, so I forced myself back onto the topic before I went too far off track in my mind. "People, huh? We're never happy, even though, deep down I think we know we are. It's as if comfort throws us off our game. We need to feel as if everything is fight or flight, so when everything is great, we throw a wrench into the works to gum it all up so it feels normal to us. Whatever normal means." I'd been dissecting that particular word a lot for months now.

"How do I stop from doing that?" She sat on her hands, and I wondered if she did so to prevent from wringing them to the point of breaking the skin on her fingers.

"You can't. Not completely, anyway. You can only minimize the damage for when you do. Don't tell Sarah or my therapist that this message has gotten through to me, or they'll expect me to be better at it than I am, but the only way to keep a relationship on balance is communication. At all times."

"Speaking of that," a guilty expression crossed Maddie's face. "I may have told Peter about your podcast before I listened to the first episode."

The thought of him hearing what I'd said felt like a knife plunging into my brain. "Has he listened?"

"He's your brother."

"That didn't answer my question." I tilted my head to one side and gave her a look that said we both knew how unpredictable the Petries could be when it came to showing the type of support other families took for granted.

"True." She offered a tiny smile. "The old Peter wouldn't have, but he's changed a lot more than you might realize. So yes, I'm pretty sure he has, and he's probably waiting for you to talk to him. The same goes for your dad."

I swallowed, my throat constricted and rough. "I know I said communication is key, but can we pretend you didn't tell me any of this?"

She snickered, but then her expression grew serious. "Sarah also knows they've listened."

"I hate you right now." I stared daggers at Maddie.

"Don't kill the messenger." She hid behind her hands, cowering. "Are you going to call them?"

"I need to process it all first." By that, I meant I needed time to figure out a way I could handle communicating with them. Maybe using a carrier pigeon or something. Dammit, why had I come out of the A-closet for all the world to see—or hear?

CHAPTER SEVENTEEN

Fred, Gandhi, and I returned from our afternoon walk, and when I checked the mailbox, there was a white plastic bag shoved into the space. I pulled it out, puzzling over the shipping label for a moment before it dawned on me what had arrived.

"They're here, Fred," I cried, a rush of excitement overtaking me. "Yippie!"

"Yips!" He raised his hands in the air, while Gandhi danced around both of us, barking.

"Let's tell the crew." I waltzed into the family room with the package held high. "They're here!"

"Yips!" Fred giggled, and it was difficult to discern if he was excited because I was or if he was tickled by the word *yips* because he pronounced it more emphatically this go around, as if he knew he was changing the true meaning of the word. Possibly both reasons planted a huge smile to his face. I absolutely adored his playfulness and the way he found joy in such simple things.

Gandhi barked, sitting on his haunches for a treat. I dug one out of my shorts pocket, tossing it in the air to him, which he caught. It was a trick we'd been working on for weeks.

"Who's here?" Sarah rushed into the room, looking frazzled. "Why didn't you tell me we were having people over?"

"We're having people over?" I repeated, totally lost. My head swiveled, searching the room. "Where are they?"

"You said it yourself," Sarah replied with a hint of exasperation. "Given your level of excitement, I assume we'll be welcoming royalty."

"When have I ever discussed wanting to meet royalty?" I pressed my lips together, making a sputtering sound. "No, it's even better than the queen coming to tea. But I have to wait until Maddie and Willow are here to announce it properly."

"Okay." Sarah boosted an eyebrow, patting Fred on the head.

Freddie whipped around, staring wide-eyed at me. Moments later, Maddie and Willow came into the room, the curiosity evident on their faces.

"Ladies, behold." I shook the contents of the bag into my hand, holding out the four boxes with a flourish. I watched expectantly for their reactions, which I was certain would be as thrilled as my own. Instead, I was met with blank faces.

"They're chunks of plastic." Maddie's facial expression was one of disappointment bordering on disgust.

"No! They're the ear swabs I ordered for everyone." After a painful second, I managed to pry one of the carrying cases open to display the swab. The tip of my finger throbbed slightly from the effort, but I bucked up, determined to persevere for the greater good. "Sarah, I got you the red one. Fred, can you help me out by giving this to your lovely mother?"

He happily skipped across the room, handing off the red carrying case, which was a skinny rectangle about half the size of a travel toothbrush.

"Maddie, you're a peach." I gave this one to Fred, who was beyond stoked to be my go-between once again.

"Careful. That could be construed as sexual harassment." Maddie leaned down and gave Fred a kiss on the cheek.

"How?" I scrunched my eyebrow. "You kissed Freddie, not me."

"I wasn't talking about kissing," Maddie said, shaking her head. "I meant calling me a peach. You know the peach emoji stands for butt, right?"

"Butt!" Freddie cried out, giggling.

"That wasn't how I—"

"Butt! Butt! Butt!"

"See what you've done?" I sighed but was determined not to let their deflated attitudes bring me to their level. Not with the fate of the planet on the line. Besides, who could get mad while Freddie danced on his tippy-toes. "Willow, you get green."

"Cool!" Her enthusiasm was genuine, and when Fred gave it to her, she let out a whistle like calling a dog, which only brought a very excited Gandhi expecting another treat. Willow obliged, of course, because she was the only other household member who carried treats in her pocket like I did. "I've been seeing ads for these everywhere and have been meaning to try one. Thanks!"

"What color did you get yourself?" Sarah asked.

"Blue," I answered.

"Trade you." Maddie held out hers. "I'm not keen on peach."

"Uh." I wasn't a fan of the color either, especially now that I equated it with butts. After a second, though, I remembered this wasn't about color preference. This was about doing my part to save the environment for my children and grandchildren. "Fine. Here."

I tossed mine through the air, and she easily caught it. The same couldn't be said for my catching abilities, but Fred pounced on it when it hit the floor and handed it to me.

"Butt."

I studied the peach rectangle with distaste.

"What if I want peach?" Sarah batted her eyelashes at me, and I knew she was simply fucking with me, but red did sound a lot better.

Then it struck me. Sarah knew I'd hate the peach one and would prefer red out of the two. She was trying to be nice. I grinned. "Deal!"

We traded, and then I tried opening the red box, which was even stiffer than the one from earlier. "There's got to be a trick to this, right?"

"Let me try." Sarah, much to my secret relief, also struggled for a second before she got hers open. It was good to know it wasn't just me. "Hmm. It looks sort of like a normal Q-tip, I guess." It was hard to ignore the doubt seeping into her tone as she inspected the small wand with its bumpy plastic tip and not a speck of cotton in sight.

"That's the whole point," I said with extra eagerness. I'll admit I may have been expecting something a little softer looking than what had arrived, but I didn't want their confused looks and doubt to infect me. "If these last us one year, that's 365 cotton swabs not being tossed in a landfill. Each! That's if you only use one per day. Some of you, and I won't name names, my eyes briefly flicked to Sarah and Maddie, use two. Times that by four people and you get..." I tapped my thumb to my fingertips on my righthand. "I'm not sure. A lot."

"That settles it. I'm putting you in charge of checking the kids' math homework." Sarah stood to kiss my cheek.

Maddie pulled her swab out of the container. "It's kinda hard, though. There's no fluffy stuff on the tips."

"Correct," I proclaimed with pride, having succeeded in convincing myself in the preceding seconds that the lack of cushiness was a good thing. "It's supposed to last and can be rinsed after each use."

"But… it's going in my ear." Maddie looked dubiously at the item. "Cotton kinda seems like a necessity."

"You can easily wash these, though," I pointed out. "Besides, it doesn't go all the way in. You're not supposed to do that with the cotton ones, either, FYI."

"I still want to get the gunk out." Maddie ran her finger over the bumpy tip of the swab. "I'll give it a go, but I'm not jumping for joy about it."

"That's the spirit!" I cheered, trying to push her negativity out of my mind. This became harder to do when I extracted mine from the case and put my finger on the unyielding plastic point. Comfort wasn't the first word that came to mind. Or the tenth. "Did you know archeologists south of London found what they believed to be a Roman device that looks remarkably like a Q-tip? They say it is somewhere between 1600 to 2000 years old, and it was made entirely of metal. Now that sounds uncomfortable. This here, though? This is nothing like metal." I placed the ends of the swab between two fingertips to show how it was more pliable, but I had to press my thumb in the middle to get it to bend ever so slightly, putting a damper on the effectiveness of my demonstration.

"You always have a historical fact up your sleeve." Sarah kissed my cheek again, which was a pretty strong indication she was trying to humor me and wasn't any more enthused about her new eco-friendly hygiene tool than Maddie was.

"Promise me you'll at least give them an honest try. It's for the kids." I patted the top of Freddie's head to hammer the point home.

"How come when I say something like that, you get mad?" Sarah's eyes crinkled with humor.

"Because you say it as a way of trying to make me eat veggies or something even more awful. Although, I'm trying to think of something more awful than veggies and am drawing a blank."

"Oh, now I see the difference." Again, she kissed my cheek. If it was possible for a kiss to contain sarcasm, I think that one might have.

"Stop doing that!" I wiped my cheek with my shoulder.

"You usually like when I kiss you."

"Not when you're mocking me or whatever you want to call it. I know the difference."

"If you don't know what to call it, how do you know the difference?" Sarah was being playful, but that didn't stop my blood pressure from rising.

"I just do!" I stormed out of the room.

"Is this about the swabs, or is there something else going on?" Maddie asked loud enough for me to hear as I entered the library.

"She's probably still upset we can't move to Mars," Sarah replied. "She really had her heart set on that."

"I wonder if aliens suck ear gunk out when they do a probe?" Maddie was laughing now.

I had to stop myself from storming back into the family room to shout, "This isn't about Mars or ear-sucking aliens!" However, after I ran the sentence through my head, I decided it was best to shut the office door and leave it be for the moment. I'd never been the type to come up with a humdinger to put someone in their place when I really needed one, and this time was no different. Usually, I came up with the perfect retort days later. I looked forward to waking up at 3:00 a.m. knowing exactly what I should've said.

So far, my conservation efforts had fallen like a lead balloon, but I couldn't give up quite yet. The future of the planet depended on humans acting less selfishly, let alone with the outright destructiveness at which our species excelled.

Sarah was partly right. Knowing Mars wasn't a viable option

made everything harder to swallow. In all my years of studying history, the main things you could count on about human behavior were greed and selfishness. If the planet truly depended on the goodness of people, it was hard to dislodge the belief that my children and grandchildren would be royally screwed, and I wouldn't be around to help. That thought practically swallowed me whole. There had to be a solution.

CHAPTER EIGHTEEN

Later that night, I crashed into the bedroom to find Sarah sitting in bed.

"Uh-oh." Sarah set her phone down. "It's never good when your eyes have that crazed look."

"I'll give you a chance to say I was right before telling you *why* I'm right." I shook the papers in my hand.

Sarah slanted her head but didn't speak, which should have been my first clue to tread lightly.

"Fine." I read the title of *The New Yorker* article to her, "'Is Mars Ours?'"

"Not Mars again," Sarah squeezed her eyes shut and dug her head into the pillow. "How did you get back on this track?"

"The how doesn't matter. This is an article about colonizing space, in a reputable publication, no less. Do you want me to read the points I've underlined?" I held the papers at eye level.

Sarah's smile faltered as she surveyed the size of the stack. "How many pages is that?"

"Five."

"If you're so concerned about the planet, why did you print the article?"

I held up my hand, shaking my head. "Don't even go that route. I printed it on the backside of other papers I've printed."

Sarah clasped her hands together, and I wasn't sure if she was saying a prayer for the trees or me. "Lizzie—"

"You always start off that way when you think I'm being unreasonable. I'm not alone in thinking the planet is beyond fucked. Elon Musk is an advocate for colonizing space."

"Elon Musk? He's a billionaire who—"

"Careful what you say." I jabbed a finger in the air. "He has Asperger's."

Sarah blinked in that way she did when whatever I'd said made her brain need to reboot. "What does that have to do with Mars?"

"Nothing, but—"

"Do you really want humanity to take their destruction to Mars?"

"I have to believe deep down that if we end up in space, after all the dedication it would take to make that happen, we'd treat it better." I sat down on the side of the bed and asked in a somewhat accusatory tone, "Did you even read the article?"

"No. You only just alerted me to it."

"Well, that part's in there. The article delves into the possibility of us wrecking it and how some believe it doesn't belong to us." My shoulders slumped, not liking to acknowledge these naysayers could have a valid point. Humans sucked, which brought me back around to the belief the best thing for the planet and solar system was our extinction. That got me nowhere in the vicinity of protecting my children, though. I massaged my eyes.

"Do you think it belongs to us?"

"I think I want my children, grandchildren, and," my brain sputtered, "what are the next ones called?"

Sarah smiled. "Great-grandchildren."

"Why are you smiling like that?" I pointed to her lips.

"Because I think it's adorable that the woman I met so many years ago, the one who went running for the hills at the prospect of us moving in together, is now staying up late to figure out a way to ensure her great-grandchildren will have decent lives." She chuckled. "If someone told me back then that this would happen, I wouldn't have believed them."

"I take my responsibilities as a parent seriously," I told her, not sure whether to take what she'd said as a compliment or a slight.

She patted my arm, which edged me toward the compliment side of the equation. "I know you do, honey. Instead of focusing on finding a new planet to inhabit, maybe we should concentrate on our family."

"Looking away isn't the solution. That's how Hitler got away with so much. Do I need to refresh your memory of Martin Niemöller's quote: *First they came for the socialists, and I did not speak out*—?"

"No." There was a tinge of desperation in Sarah's eyes as she quickly responded. "I haven't forgotten, and looking away entirely isn't what I'm suggesting. You like steps. Let's start with the first step." She raised a finger in the air, capturing my full attention.

"What's that?" I perked up, looking forward to whatever insight she was about to impart.

"It's time for bed."

My shoulders sagged again. "That's not a viable step to saving the planet."

"It's a step for stopping you from collapsing from exhaustion, and I have a killer headache after Ollie screamed non-stop for thirty minutes right before bed."

"She did?" I fought a yawn but unsuccessfully.

"You see!" Sarah crowed.

I narrowed my eyes. "It's after ten. Of course, I'm tired. It's not like you solved a mystery or something."

"Yes, dear. Solving problems is your thing." Sarah scooted down, her body now hidden under the covers. "Can you solve things with the lights out?"

"I'm not in the mood for *that*."

Sarah's eyelids flew open, but they quickly slitted to barely visible, which never boded well. "What makes you think I'm even offering *that*?"

"Uh..." I started to set the papers on her nightstand but thought better of it because I wanted to reread them in the morning when my brain was fresh. I didn't want them to go *missing*, which was basically code for Sarah throwing them out when I wasn't looking.

Unfortunately, Sarah wasn't a fool. "Are you afraid I'll burn them?"

"I hadn't put much thought into how you'd destroy them, but I like to keep these things just in case." I hefted a shoulder.

"In case...?" She scooted upright again.

"I need to remind you that you're wrong, and I'm right."

Sarah's eyes closed, and she sucked in a deep breath, slowly letting it out. "So, what you're saying is you have a file of *evidence*"—she made quote marks in the air—"about how I'm wrong?"

"Not just *one* file." Damn, I wished I hadn't let that slip out.

Sarah cradled her forehead with her palm. "Sometimes, I don't know what to say to you. Go, file your paperwork. I'm too tired to argue, and I'm done talking."

"But—"

She motioned with her hand that I should close my trap, so I did, but in my head, I was making counterpoint on top of counterpoint as to how it was wrong of her to tell me to shut up when I wanted to talk things through. It really didn't make me feel appreciated or seen. How many times had she begged me to open up more? So many times I couldn't remember them all. But now when I wanted to discuss a situation, she shut me down.

I started to open my mouth to point all of this out, but she gave me a death stare that topped all others, so I left the bedroom and headed for my office, but I stopped in the kitchen to get a Fudgsicle because now I was getting a tremendous headache and I'd heard they helped. Might as well try. What was the worst that could happen?

CHAPTER NINETEEN

I woke early the following morning, confused as to why I was on the library couch with a pile of popsicle sticks on the coffee table next to an empty yellow Fudgsicle box.

Had someone drugged me in my sleep and force-fed me enough chocolate ice cream treats to choke a horse?

That didn't sound plausible, even to me, and as the sleepiness receded from my brain, the pounding in my head brought back recollections of the night before. I'd tried to get my sinus headache under control by following an online tip I'd come across. Apparently, after the first failed attempt, I tried it four more times.

I wasn't the type to quit easily.

Sarah, wearing a robe and fuzzy slippers, walked into the room and arched an eyebrow at the fudgsicle mess. She pursed her lips but didn't say a word.

I cradled my head. "It hurts."

"Are you sure it's not brain freeze from all the ice cream?" she asked dryly. Her expression changed to one of sympathy as she sat down on the couch, wrapping an arm around me. "We need to figure out the solution to your headaches."

"The doctor said I need to drink more water."

"You already drink plenty. Soon, you'll reach camel status." She flicked a hand to the empty box. "Do I want to know about those?"

"Someone recommended them to me as a headache solution."

"Did it help?"

"I ended up falling asleep, so there's that." I glanced down at my T-shirt. "We'll need to stock up on stain remover."

Sarah laughed.

"Are you still mad at me?"

"No. Are you still mad?"

"I'm not sure," I said, trepidation making me choose my words carefully. "I don't feel like you or the other seven billion people realize how fucked this planet is. We brought children into this world. My job is to protect them. Even when I'm gone—"

"Lizzie, don't talk that way. You aren't going anytime soon." She tightened her grip on me, rocking us ever so slightly.

"Let's hope that's the case, but it doesn't change the fact that the threat to the planet is real."

"Of course, it doesn't. I understand that, and to apologize for overreacting last night, I purchased some net bags for when we buy produce."

My lips twitched into a half-smile. "You did?"

"Yes."

"Did you click the no-rush delivery option?" I pressed, not willing to take the victory without pushing for a little more. "Not only does it help, but I also get a buck for a digital product. I've got my eye on a book about Musk."

"Is it called *Liftoff*?"

"Yes. How'd you know?" I squinted one eye, trying to remember if I'd mentioned it before, but I'd been careful to avoid playing my hand considering the resistance I'd gotten about colonizing Mars. Not only that, but I already had so much on my plate with research for the classes I taught and now for the podcast, too. Proclaiming I had taken on an additional massive research project didn't seem like the brightest idea, especially considering I hadn't known about Ollie's bedtime meltdown until Sarah told me two hours after the fact.

"I ordered you a copy. I know you prefer marking up the margins with a pen." She leaned over and kissed my forehead.

Some of my tension eased, but not all, like I still expected the other shoe to drop. "Why'd you buy it?"

"Let's just say I felt guilty shooing you away last night."

"I probably could have handled it better." As evidence of that, I tugged on the front of my shirt, the ice cream stain was chunky and starting to smell.

"We both could have. Would you like some tea?"

I looked at her suspiciously. "Are you really not going to yell at me?"

"For wanting a cup of tea?"

"For starting another massive project and for admitting I keep files about the times you were wrong."

Her chuckle wasn't brimming with humor so much as it seemed to be resignation. "I can't stop you when you put your mind to something. Besides, you're determined enough you might do something that saves all of us."

"Now, I know you're buttering me up. I can't do simple math without a calculator, but I do have an ace up my sleeve."

She gazed at me with such intensity, and I couldn't determine if the thoughts going through her head were good or bad. Either way, it was probably best to drop the Mars thread, so I said, "Let's get tea and coffee going."

CHAPTER TWENTY

I WAS IN MY OFFICE, prepping for one of my fall classes when Ethan rang through on Skype. The start of the new semester was still weeks away, but my brain didn't like putting things off to the last minute, and I was about to reject his call when I remembered it might be Casey to discuss Operation Mars.

My niece, not a true blood relation but one I liked even more than most of my so-called legit peeps, was the ace up my sleeve I'd hinted to Sarah about, though I hadn't shared the details.

"Hey there," I said as Ethan's image appeared on my screen, trying to hide my disappointment as I spied the narrow moustache and coke-bottle glasses that most definitely did not belong to Casey. "To what do I owe the pleasure?"

He gave me an odd, searching look. "We got a big package from Amazon today. Know anything about that?"

I couldn't tell if he was angry, confused, or humored by this, so I hedged my bets. "Did you open the box? I find that helps. Unless you think it's a bomb or something. If that's the case, call the authorities."

"Very funny, wise guy." He held up a collection of Robert A. Heinlein books, which of course I recognized but wasn't quite ready to let on. "There's also a telescope and a biography on Elon Musk's quest to reach Mars. So, I repeat, know anything about it?" He motioned for me to fill in the blank.

"Oh that!" I bonked my forehead in what may have been a slightly melodramatic attempt to appear nonchalant. "Yeah, Casey and I got to talking the other day—"

"Don't blame my daughter for this, and while I love it when you take an interest—"

I didn't want him to slam the door before I had a chance to plead my case, so I blurted, "She's brilliant, and I need help with my project. I didn't know who else to call."

"I got that much out of Casey already." He let out a sigh—possibly in exasperation—as he massaged his temples and stared into the camera. "Let me see if I'm understanding your objective. You want my daughter, who isn't in high school yet, to figure out a way to move you and your children to Mars?"

No, not exasperation. Disbelief.

I set my pen down, knowing this call was going to take longer than I'd hoped. "Yes and no. It's a bit more nuanced than you make it sound."

"This I can't wait to hear." He crossed his arms over his chest. "Please, go on."

"Sarah told me moving to Mars wasn't a possibility, but I've been doing some research, and there are plenty of smart people out there who think it is. But you know science isn't my strong suit. After all, I got a B in astronomy."

"So, you think my daughter can help you with the hard parts?" It was difficult to determine if he was baffled or proud.

"I'm not expecting her to build a spaceship or anything, but I do think she can help me understand the material. Actually, I thought she was the one calling me. Not you. Otherwise, I wouldn't have answered."

Ethan started to laugh, his upper body moving up and down in a herky-jerky fashion, which is about the point it hit me that what I'd said might have been blunter than I'd intended. "I do miss your antics. Why is Sarah being mean and telling you Mars is out of the question?"

"I think she's worried I'll get my hopes up, and then it'll crush me if it doesn't come to fruition."

"I'm with Sarah on this one." The smile slipped off his face, replaced by caution or possibly concern.

My spirits deflated as I considered what his next move would be. "Does that mean you're taking Casey off my team?"

"Not at all," he said, which reassured me somewhat, "especially if you continue to send presents. I haven't read all of Heinlein yet, so by all means, keep 'em coming. It's been hard getting books from the library during this never-ending plague. It's like everyone suddenly rediscovered reading, which is great, but all the books I want to check out have long waiting lists."

"I'm sorry, Ethan. Not about the waiting lists," I clarified and frowned. "Well, yeah, about the lists, too. That sucks. But what I meant was I should have asked before speaking to Casey about working on a project with me."

"All I have to say is it's a shame you don't live here anymore because then you could be the one to get up in the middle of the night to check out some celestial event next week." Despite what he'd said, his smile was back, and there was a spark in his eyes that reassured me, though being able to read subtle social cues was far from one of my strengths.

"For a man complaining, you don't seem all that upset." I slanted my head to the right, and then left, doing my best to gauge his true thoughts, but it was harder with a video call that continued to become fuzzy whenever the wind blew because my WiFi acted up.

"Honestly, Casey and I are bonding over this project you've

initiated," Ethan admitted, which I was glad to hear. "I've always wanted to learn more about constellations and stuff."

"I remember you wearing a Dune shirt to one of the twins' parties."

"One question." Ethan's face took on a mischievous look as he leaned closer to the camera. "What do I get out of this deal?"

I was about to ask what he wanted, a knee-jerk reaction when I felt like something more was expected of me, but then it struck me. "Didn't you say you and Casey are bonding? Isn't that enough? Personally, I think you should be grateful to have an interest in common with your child."

I started to wonder which of my kids would be the scientist. Fred loved learning things and banging the drums, while Ollie was sportier. Demi definitely had the artistic gene. So far, I'd determined Cal, who preferred his stroller or being carried, would be the type to run a hedge fund simply so he could afford servants to take care of mundane things like walking. I could kind of picture him being carried around like Cleopatra. What would I end up having in common with them?

Ethan was still giving me that evil look, the one that said he had leverage over me that I had yet to consider. "I'm thinking you don't want me to tell Sarah about how your master plan involves child labor."

"Casey loves to read and explore!" I squeezed my thigh, trying to curb my emotions. What a totally far-fetched accusation. It didn't matter, though. Sarah wouldn't like it one bit.

"I know, but I can spin it just right to get you up shit's creek without a paddle." He acted out paddling, which didn't make sense because the phrase mentioned not having one.

"You wouldn't dare!" I shook a finger at the camera so he'd be able to pick up my ferocity. After adding a grunting sort of growl to my repertoire, I crossed my arms and stared daggers at him. "Let's suppose you're right, and I don't want Sarah to find out all the details of this little project. What will it cost me?"

He scratched his head, pretending to think, but there was little doubt in my mind he'd gone into this call with the intent to extort. "I've always wanted the complete Robert A. Heinlein collection."

My eyes narrowed. "This is blackmail."

"Such an ugly word." He tsked as if I was the one in the wrong.

I made a show of mulling it over, but the decision was obvious. As much as I didn't like being fleeced, I enjoyed a tongue lashing from my wife even less. "Fine. Email me a list of all the books you need to finish your set."

"Always a pleasure doing business with you."

"Hey." I could tell he was about to hang up, so I waved for him to wait. "You didn't listen to my demand yet."

"Your demand?" Ethan looked taken aback. "Why do you think you get one?"

I pressed my lips together to suppress a grin, which I feared would end up being a little too much on the evil side. "Because if I tell Lisa—"

"You wouldn't dare!" It was his turn to act indignant.

"Oh, but I might." It was only fair, even if Ethan's living arrangement with his wife and her girlfriend was different from the norm. To be clear, Ethan wasn't in a throuple, but they all lived in the same house to raise Casey. While it was difficult for the likes of me to comprehend, it wasn't like I had a normal family, either. "Once you hear what I'm asking, I think you'll decide it's not worth taking the risk to find out."

He raked his hand across his head, not enjoying the way the tables had turned nearly as much as I was. "Okay. Hit me with it."

"Calvin spilled red juice on my white CSU shirt." I folded

my arms across my chest, roughly where the aforementioned juice had landed, breaking my heart. "I want a new one."

"You can order one online, can't you?"

"Not the same kind." Did he think I hadn't checked? This was my favorite shirt we were talking about. "I prefer the one that's only sold at the student center."

"Of course, you do. Do you miss it? The campus, not the shirt?" His voice softened, and it touched me that he knew he needed to clarify for me. Ethan was one of the few who always got me, even when I didn't get myself.

"I do miss it, very much," I admitted, the dull ache of homesickness settling like a weight on my chest. "The Wellesley campus is beautiful, but there's something special about CSU."

"Do you ever think you'll move back?"

"Never say never." I sighed, willing myself to ignore that little bit of sadness I couldn't shake as I contemplated how unlikely it was. "Not anytime soon, though. We like exploring out here now that we can leave the house. I'm hoping you guys will be able to visit at some point, when things aren't so apocalyptic."

"Maybe when Casey figures out the Mars dilemma, we can all go back to normal, whatever that will be like on Mars."

"I have all the confidence in the world in your daughter," I declared, truly meaning it. If our planet was going to get out of the mess we were in, it would be up to the younger generation to figure it out. Casey might as well get a head start.

I was certain Ethan agreed as his proud papa grin practically leapt off my screen. "You've always been a good aunt."

"Besides," I added before I could consider whether what I was saying was wise, which it probably wasn't, "I hate losing anything. Casey simply has to figure out Mars so I can prove Sarah wrong."

"Well, it sounds like you have your priorities straight." He let his southern accent really drawl.

I offered a sly grin. "I've always got my eye on the prize."

"That you do. I gotta jump, or Casey will have my head. She hates being late to science camp."

He disappeared, and I wondered if he had intended to quiz me about the A-word and forgotten or if he hadn't listened to my podcast yet.

CHAPTER TWENTY-ONE

After my Skype call, I returned my attention to the fall lecture I was prepping. Summertime was the best because I could get ahead of schedule. I was so engrossed in what I was doing that the first time I became aware I wasn't alone was when Sarah stood in front of my desk, waving her arms. I jumped in my chair with a start, my heart racing as I eased my headphones off my ears.

"Earth to Lizzie!" she said, doing her best to imitate the sound of ground control coming through a speaker in space. "I've been calling your name for five minutes."

"Sorry. What's up?" It took some effort, but I set the book down and gave her my full attention, only sneaking one or two longing glances at most.

"It's almost time for dinner."

"O-okay." I wasn't following. If it was only almost time, that meant it wasn't actually time yet, and I could have gotten in another page or two, maybe more. "Do I need to set the table?"

"No." The way she looked at me made it clear I was missing something really obvious that she'd probably told me earlier when I wasn't paying attention. When I still didn't get it after several seconds, she tossed her hands up in the air. "You need to pick it up, Lizzie. Remember? I ordered. You promised to pick up."

"Oh!" I leapt to my feet, the conversation I'd been only vaguely aware of while my head was mostly in Mars rushing back to me in much greater detail. "You got it!"

"You're pretty excited to run an errand," Sarah remarked with a laugh. "I thought you'd whine and try to claim your lecture was something you had to finish."

"Are you kidding me? After being cooped up in the house for a year, it seems like such a novelty to pick up takeout. Kinda like the good old days." Which was not to say I wouldn't have tried to pull a stunt like the one Sarah had suggested.

"I'm thrilled not to have to cook every single meal. I cannot wait to sit inside a restaurant again. Seriously, I can't wait!" She grinned like a child asking Santa for a Star Wars Lego set.

"Do I need to go anywhere else?" I rubbed my hands together greedily, hoping for an excuse to stop somewhere, anyplace. "Maybe the kids need shoes, or I could get some groceries, or—"

"All we need is dinner. Don't go overboard like you do with everything else." On her way out of the library, Sarah called over her shoulder, "Speaking of, I heard Casey got a new telescope."

"I can't believe Ethan ratted me out!" I slammed a fist into my palm. "I gave into his blackmail and everything."

Sarah, who had reached the doorway, stopped in her tracks and slowly turned around. "What did you say?"

Dammit!

For all I knew, she didn't know a thing about Operation Mars. Maybe she'd only heard about the telescope and assumed I'd sent it as a gift. But now I'd stupidly mentioned blackmail and opened the door to a Sarah Inquisition. I definitely didn't deserve that. Or, probably not.

Maybe.

I mean, Ethan had already talked with me about the way I'd overstepped the aunt-niece relationship boundaries by keeping him out of the loop when recruiting Casey. That seemed like sufficient scolding for what was nothing more than a minor infraction at most. Honestly, I didn't even think he'd been mad about it. He only called me out because he knows how to play me to get shit.

But was that how Sarah was going to see this? I'd have to find out eventually, but fortunately for me, I currently had a *get out of jail free* card.

"I better go get dinner. We don't want it getting cold, and I'm starving." I rubbed my belly, not liking how it protruded more than usual. Making it go away was even higher on my list than getting to Mars, but it was proving equally as difficult. I knew exercise was key—along with drinking more water, as I'd discovered on a fitness blog recently—but no way was I going there and letting my doctor have the last laugh. Unfortunately, I hadn't figured out a way to listen to an audiobook and take notes while riding my bike. Besides, finding bike trails without Masshole drivers was proving difficult.

The whole time I'd been lost in my head, Sarah had been staring me down. Now, she crossed her arms and gave me her *confess or die* glare. "What? Did? You? Do?"

"It's pretty intimidating when you turn each word into a question in that tone, ya know," I muttered, sounding guiltier with every syllable. "I don't exactly appreciate it."

She continued to stare at me, meaning my attempted guilt trip didn't have the desired effect.

Fuck.

"It's no biggie," I insisted, wishing I'd been a little quicker to make my exit. If only I'd remembered about the dinner pickup on my own, I could've been on the road already instead of in hot water with Sarah. From now on, I was going to create a reminder on my phone for absolutely everything. "I simply sent Casey a telescope because she asked for one, but I didn't run it by Ethan first."

"Was he mad?" Something told me she didn't outright think I was lying, but she didn't believe every word I'd said either. At least, I felt reassured I'd provided enough details that matched the knowledge she already possessed, and her suspicions hadn't dramatically increased.

"I'd say he was more amused than mad," I told her, which was true. Amused and greedy. "He and Casey are camping this weekend to observe some celestial event, which I should get credit for, really. Ethan's as nerdy as Casey, although he doesn't want to admit it."

"I suppose you did a good deed, then." She still didn't sound entirely convinced, but I refused to speak another word unless asked a direct question on the topic since I had a habit of overdoing it with smoke screens. Less is more, a concept I always seemed to forget. "That reminds me. Freddie needs a new Buzz Lightyear. Ollie smashed his."

"Why doesn't that surprise me? I'll order one when I get home." Realizing the potential for more out-of-the-house time, I added, "Or should I stop at a toy store and see if they have one in stock?"

"I don't think it qualifies as a *go into the store during a pandemic* emergency."

"People should take space emergencies more seriously!" I cringed at how loudly I'd spoken. I hadn't intended to be so forceful, thoroughly wrecking my lame joke.

Again, Sarah raked me with her intense stare, clearly seeking to rattle my nerves to get me to spill, but I wasn't going to this time. It was too important. Humanity was in a break-glass level of environmental emergency, but no one on the planet, most of this household included, gave two shits about how dire things were going to become. All that did was put more pressure on me to find a solution.

CHAPTER TWENTY-TWO

"What sociopath puts peas and carrots in fried rice?" I started sorting the veggies into a pile on the edge of my plate, practically losing my shit when the peas continued to roll off the lip back toward the center, touching what I deemed to be acceptable food. "This never happened with the Chinese place in Fort Collins."

"It's obvious, isn't it? The ones in Wellesley have it out for you." Sarah scooped the veggies onto Calvin's high chair without sparing so much as a glance in my direction, let alone any sympathy for my plight. "He loves his veggies. Don't you, Cal?"

He plucked at one of the peas with his chubby fingers, popping it into his mouth, making happy sounds as if they truly were delicious.

"I think I'm going to barf." I closed my eyes to stop the bile from rising.

"I know you're super sensitive about food, but not all of our kids are, so..." Sarah did her best not to sound judgmental, although letting her voice trail off possibly negated her neutrality.

"Yeah, I know. Everyone I have ever shared a meal with has told me. Not to mention, my mother used to spray me down with a hose after the meals when she force-fed me green peas, making me spit them out or vomit."

Sarah held her chopsticks right below her mouth, possibly so dumbfounded she'd temporarily forgotten how to move her arm. "She actually did that?"

"She said she did, but I was only two or maybe three, so I don't remember. It was one of her favorite stories to share with dinner guests, causing lots of laughter. *At* me, not *with* me. In case you weren't sure."

She set her chopsticks down, the bite uneaten. "The more I learn about her—I didn't think it was possible to like her less, but I do. I'm sorry, Lizzie. No child should have been treated that way."

"Luckily, Dad hired a nanny around then, I think. My memories are harder to pin down the older I get. Not that he ever said anything to me, but I'm pretty sure he was worried I wouldn't survive the Scotch-lady's child-rearing methods." I ruffled the top of Demi's head as she sat on my left. "None of our children will ever be treated that way. Right, my little Demitasse? Each of you is precious, quirks and all."

"Quirks!" she squealed before sucking in a lo mein noodle with a satisfactory slurp.

Ollie hammered down a teriyaki skewer, but Fred hadn't eaten so much as a single bite of any of the food on his plate. I met Sarah's eye, and she nodded that she'd already taken note of that fact, too.

I got to my feet and pulled out a hot dog from a compartment in the fridge. I placed it on a plate and nuked it in the microwave. "When in doubt, feed the boy a hot dog."

Sarah laughed, "He really is your mini-you."

That was what worried me. From the reading I'd been doing, food aversion was a major sign of autism. Had I passed the A-word on to him? It overwhelmed me with guilt. Sure, I'd learned to get through life fine with it, but that didn't mean I wanted to saddle my son with something that would make his life harder. If I'd known…

Sarah must have noticed the extent to which that thought was weighing on my shoulders because when I set the hot dog on Freddie's plate, she took the opportunity to say, "There's nothing wrong with you, or with…" She jerked her eyes to Fred, who held the hot dog with one hand, taking the tiniest bite after giving it a good sniff first and then poking it with his tongue to ensure it wasn't piping hot. Two more traits we shared: sniffing and temp checks.

What had I done?

"You're positive about that? Because I'm pretty sure you want to wring my neck roughly every third mealtime. My list of approved foods is minimal at best." I sat back down and continued plucking the peas and carrots from my fried rice, illustrating my point.

"We've never been to a restaurant where you haven't been able to find something on the menu you'll eat."

"Would you spray me with a hose if I puked up something you made me eat?"

"Two things." Sarah's tone was firm and unwavering. "First, I wouldn't force you to eat anything. Second, if for some reason you did end up getting sick, I would find a more appropriate way to clean you off. I'm not barbaric. Honestly, I don't understand how your mom could have been so mean to one of her children."

I nodded, sucking in a fortifying breath. "I don't think I ever had a chance with that woman. No matter how hard I tried to please her, she never was going to like me. Being a lesbian and—"

"Screw her!" Sarah banged her palm on the table, not even

letting me finish my list of reasons my mother had hated me. Sarah didn't usually swear in front of the kids, but one glance at the anger flaring in her eyes told me she'd probably toned down her word choice as much as she could in the heat of the moment.

That didn't stop Ollie from chanting, "Screw her!" right when Rose and Troy appeared in the kitchen. Awesome.

"What'd Lizzie do now?" Rose quipped.

"Oh, we were talking about her mother." Sarah made a *whoopsie daisy* face and said, "We're running a bit late for ice cream. Would you like any Chinese?"

Rose shook her head, but Troy grabbed a plate.

"We're going for ice cream?" I asked.

"Yeah, the cow place. Your fave." Sarah winked.

"Just what the day was missing," I grumbled, still feeling out of sorts from my walk down memory lane. "There's nothing quite like cows pissing in a field."

"Nice try, Lizzie," Sarah cajoled. "You can't fool me. Underneath that crusty exterior, I can see the light in your eyes at the thought of ice cream."

"Their chocolate peanut butter ice cream is probably the best I've tried. I would like it noted it pains me to admit that." I pounded the side of my fist into my chest with the drama of a Shakespearean actor.

"You really are the bravest." There was a smile on Sarah's lips, but her eyes showed hints of sadness, too. Whenever I shared yet another tidbit from the childhood I'd endured with my family, I think it chiseled off a piece of her heart. I didn't want to hurt her, yet I couldn't seem to stop talking about it lately. My recent project of tallying up all the things my mother did because she didn't understand I wasn't exactly normal, whatever that meant, had raised my awareness too much to let it go anymore. Part of me could see how overly self-absorbed completing my list actually was, but it also helped me realize all the things that'd been done wrong for someone like me. Not that it could change anything, but perhaps it would help me come to terms with the abuse and ensure my parenting skills far exceeded my own experiences.

CHAPTER TWENTY-THREE

That night, when I crawled into bed with Sarah, she set her book down on the side table and looked pointedly in my direction. "Why are you avoiding phone calls with your dad?"

Immediately, I shriveled like a raisin under the accusation, even though I had no idea what she meant. "I wasn't aware I was doing that. I remember him calling the other day, but I was in the middle of a podcast recording, so I rejected the call. I'd meant to return it, but I spaced that task."

"Is that the truth?" She met my eyes. "It wasn't intentional?"

"Why would I lie about it?" I scooted down under the covers, getting cozy. While the temps outside hung in the upper eighties with loads of humidity, the AC unit hummed in the corner, making me chilly.

"You lie?" Sarah let out a short, staccato laugh. "That's an absurd thought. Or is it?"

My stomach tightened at the implied accusation in her question. "Now, I really don't know what you mean."

"I mean, why did you lie about the reason for buying a telescope for Casey?" Sarah took a quick breath. "Don't try to deny it."

Seriously? I should've known Ethan couldn't last an entire day without squealing. I was about to say as much when another possibility stopped me. Was Sarah fishing? She was sneaky like that. I groaned over the fact I was the one being cagey. Sarah had boatloads of experience to know when I wasn't being completely upfront. She could probably see through me right now. The best way out of this conversation was to go back to what had kicked it off.

"Do I need to call my dad right now?" I started to toss the covers off of me, ready to do just that.

"No, he got ahold of me when you didn't call. He's on his way here to talk to you," Sarah said, like it was a perfectly natural thing for him to do, and maybe it would've been if we hadn't moved across the country.

I gaped at her. "Does he not remember we moved to Massachusetts?"

"Pretty sure he does." She shook her head in the way that blared I was the one with a loose screw.

"There's a pandemic," I argued, my voice becoming shrill with worry. "He's in a vulnerable population. Why is he traveling?"

"He's fully vaxxed, and so are we, finally," Sarah reminded me, not that it made me feel at all better. Even vaccines weren't one-hundred percent guarantees that nothing bad would happen. "He hasn't seen you or his grandchildren in over a year. This is the summer of grandparent hugs."

"Is that the only reason he's coming?" My question was laced with suspicion. Somehow, I couldn't see my dad as a *travel across the country for a hug* type of guy. There had to be an ulterior motive.

"Between you and me, I think he's up to something big."

She spoke in a conspiratorial tone, her eyes furtively moving around the room.

"I knew it." Even after saying this with the utmost conviction, I remained baffled. "What is it?"

"Oh, I don't know. Maybe he's considering hiring a child to lead the way to colonizing Mars."

"Goddammit. I'm going to kill Ethan." I pulled the comforter up to my chin, not simply because I was cold, but Sarah's glare was sharp enough to leave marks on my bare skin.

She feigned innocence. "What does he have to do with this?"

"Is this a trick question?" I'm not sure why I bothered asking. I knew the answer, and my goose was cooked on this one.

"What I can't figure out is if both of you put this idea in Casey's head?" Sarah crossed her arms over her chest.

"Hold on a minute. Something isn't adding up. Who told you I've steered Casey into studying Mars and the possibility of space travel?"

"Casey did. We've been texting."

"Casey has a phone?" How had I missed that milestone? "She isn't old enough for a phone, is she?

"But she's old enough to figure out how the human race can colonize Mars?" Sarah scoffed. "Honest to God, Lizzie. I don't know what you're thinking half the time. But no. To answer your question, she texts via her Kindle Fire."

"So, the other day in my off—the library, when you asked me about the telescope, you already knew the answer." This was a statement, not a question, and it may have had a harsh tone to it because I was still smarting from the way Sarah had so thoroughly exposed the weak points of my plan. "That's not nice."

Sarah quirked her right eyebrow and stared at me for a good

three seconds before I started to wilt. "I really hate it when you do that."

"Do you mean when I catch you in a lie, or when I call you out on being an idiot?"

"Both." I stuck my tongue out at her.

"I don't know why you felt like you had to obfuscate."

"You flat out told me not to pin my hopes on Mars. I had to get creative."

"Honestly? I don't think it should be your sole reason for going on, no."

"Is there a but coming?" I groaned. "There is, isn't there?"

"I'm not sure about that. However—"

"*However* is a different form of saying *but*."

"Stop interrupting, please. What I was going to say is Casey loves the project." Sarah didn't say anything else, leaving me hanging.

"And…?" Was I in trouble or not?

"I can see Freddie taking to it when he's old enough. He loves to build things. Maybe he'll build you your very own spaceship since you're not big on sharing."

"I hadn't thought of that." I ran my hand through my hair, contemplating the possibility. "He's pretty smart and has the temperament of a genius."

"No pressure, then." Sarah laughed. "I'm not opposed to you studying the subject, and I think it's cute you and Casey have a not-so-secret mission. It's got to be hard for her, being so smart and not having a lot of friends her own age to talk to, though goodness knows you're basically a big kid."

"I know what that's like, being the odd one out." I released a heavy sigh, ignoring Sarah's comment about me being childish. Now was not the time to argue that point. My Disney pajamas weren't a ringing endorsement of my adulthood.

"You mean the friends part?"

"Did you just slam me somehow?" I closed one of my eyes, trying to figure out how. Was she implying I wasn't smart? Or maybe too smart for my own good? I was really confused.

"You can't prove anything." Her expression sparkled with gaiety.

"Don't be cruel."

"I'm not," she said softly. "I'm sorry. I really didn't intend anything as a slam, you know. Sometimes, I like teasing you."

"Why?"

"Because you're loveable when you pout." She kissed my cheek.

"It's not fair."

"What isn't?" she whispered in my ear.

The hair on my neck stood up, in a good way. A very good way. "You're doing this on purpose."

"That's wrong of me?" Sarah licked my earlobe, making me wriggle.

"You're trying to make me feel better after insinuating I'm not a genius and that I don't have friends."

"You don't like people, though. I'm not sure how you can be upset about not having friends when you go out of your way not to make any. You do like this." Sarah rolled on top of me, pinning my arms above my head.

I stared into her eyes, forgetting all the reasons I was upset, but I still said, "You're cheating."

"Punish me, then." The longing in her eyes burned with hot intensity.

"You're incorrigible."

She responded with her killer smile, the one that did things to me that made me lose all ability to speak. I kissed her. Hungry and hard. Sarah met my enthusiasm, kicking it up a hundredfold.

Soon, our limbs were entangled as we rushed to get

undressed, wanting to feel our skin on the other. This had come out of nowhere, yet it felt almost like if we didn't come together immediately, we'd perish.

Sarah's teeth sank into my neck just hard enough to make me moan.

My fingers dug into her back, pulling her close.

She worked her way down to my right nipple, taking it into her mouth. I ran my hands up and down her bare back. Her mouth continued its downward trek, lighting up my insides.

"How do you do this to me?" I asked, my hands grabbing onto the pillow under my head.

"I could say the same to you." She peered up at me with those stunning dark eyes, and I welcomed their ability to pierce my armor.

As she watched every reaction of mine, she slipped a finger inside me, and my entire body clenched.

Moving in and out of me, she continued to observe my every reaction, smiling in that way of hers that proclaimed only she knew what I needed. It was true. Sarah always had a way of soothing my overworked mind to allow me to sink into the moment and enjoy the good parts of life. Making love was at the top of that list.

She added another finger, going in deeper.

I closed my eyes, unable to focus on anything else but the way she made me feel.

Before I knew it, she lapped my clit, sensuously and slowly.

While we'd started out frantic, Sarah switched gears, taking her time to demonstrate how much she enjoyed fucking me. It was impossible to think of anything else hotter than this sexy woman wanting me. Even after all the shit we've been through. All the times I wasn't fully honest or didn't know how to express myself. No matter what, Sarah always loved me, and she seemed to understand why I reacted to things in my very

Lizzie way, even when I didn't comprehend all of my motivations.

I reached for her left hand, our wedding rings clinking, and I knew no matter what, Sarah and I would grow old together.

CHAPTER TWENTY-FOUR

ONE WEEK LATER, I paced the kitchen with my cup of Earl Grey in hand, my eyes continually flicking to the red numbers on the microwave as they ticked closer to one in the afternoon. I felt like an animal trapped in a zoo, traveling the same path over and over with no escape.

"Here I thought you'd be hiding in the library all day." Sarah joined me in the kitchen and poured herself a fresh cup of coffee. Neither of us had slept much the previous night due to my tossing and turning. Despite that, she looked amazing, as she always did. I was pretty sure my hair was standing up in tufts all over my head.

"I don't hide."

Sarah snorted, her way of saying she thought what I'd said was total BS, without having to come out and say it.

"The library is my office," I argued, growing whiny, "and I happen to work a lot." I really wanted to stomp my foot but didn't, and I'd like to point out how unfair it is that I showed restraint and got zero credit for it. That's the problem with restraint. The absence of throwing a fit never gets proper acknowledgement.

"Work is one of your methods of hiding," she said sweetly, like a cartoon princess who was about to be surrounded by happy forest creatures singing songs. "You know it as well as I do. Would you like me to point out other ways you hole up so you don't have to deal with things you don't want to?"

"No, that's not what I need in this exact moment."

What I needed was... I honestly didn't know. A drink would've been nice, if only I hadn't sworn off the stuff. According to the clock, my father and Helen were due to arrive in twenty minutes. Being fully sober seemed like a terrible idea under the circumstances.

"What do you need, then?" She put up a hand to stop me and said, "Don't say a rocket ship."

Sometimes, it is uncanny how well that woman knows me.

"Come on. A rocket would be helpful. Not simply as a way of leaving this effed-up planet, which I truly think we're going to need, but when houseguests arrive, I could blast off to space." I let out a longing sigh. "That would be so nice."

Sarah leaned against the counter. "Before we moved, you were getting along with your father. What's changed?"

"We didn't know about me being... *you know*," I whispered, glancing over my shoulders to see if Rose, who was with the kids in the front room, might've heard.

"Honey, you announced it on your podcast. Everyone knows now."

"I don't like that." I took a step back, bumping into the counter behind me, feeling even more trapped.

"Then why did—?" She stopped with that thought, turning back to the other topic. "Never mind. Your father has known you all his life. I'm pretty sure finding out you're autistic won't change the way he feels about you."

"But it's changing me and how I feel about things." I set my mug down, already regretting opening my mouth.

"Talk to me, please." There was no way she was letting this drop now.

The problem with trapped animals in cages is they eventually lash out. I was no different. "Why is it when you want me to talk about something, you insist I should, but when I want to talk, you get to play the *I'm too tired* card?"

I could visibly see her effort to control her first retort. Perhaps her second and third as well. Finally, she was able to say, "Considering your father is driving two thousand miles to see you, I think it's best we discuss why you don't want to see him before he arrives."

"It might have been better if we'd had this conversation *before* you invited him." I stepped up on my tippy-toes, which was technically not a foot stomp, so it still qualified as showing restraint. But would anyone pat me on the back about it? Oh, no.

"Maybe you should answer your phone when those who care about you call so I don't have to be the middle person." She steadied her breathing, and I had to hand it to her. When she needed to be extra patient, she simply willed herself to be. The only tell that she was getting frustrated was the way her teeth clenched, making her jaw bulge a little beneath her ears. For some strange reason, focusing on that calmed me a little.

"What do I say to him?"

She slanted her head. "What do you want to say to him?"

That was a classic therapist move if I'd ever seen one, but I fell for it anyway. Maybe I was tired of struggling, or I needed to talk more than I wanted to admit. "I want to know why."

"Why what?"

"Why I didn't matter enough to save me from a terrible mother? Was I not lovable? Is that it? He found Helen, helped raise Gabe, and then they had Allen. Was I too much for my father to handle, and it was easier to let me drown?" I balled one of my hands into a fist and slammed it against my thigh.

Everything was coming out in a rush, and there was no stopping it even if I'd wanted to. I swallowed, choking a bit but barreling on. "When I look at our kids, I know deep down I'd walk through fire to save them."

"Of course, you would," Sarah agreed. She didn't even point out that she would do the same because I knew it was true. She stayed quiet, and something told me Sarah wasn't stewing about not getting credit for her restraint. Not like I would've been.

There had to be something really wrong with me.

Tears were threatening to spill down my cheeks, but I pressed on. "I must not have mattered to him then, and I'm having a hard time seeing me ever really taking precedence in his life. I guess it doesn't matter anymore. I'm married with four kids. I live in a different state. Why would he start being a father to me now? Honestly, I know you think it's a long shot, but figuring out a way to colonize Mars seems less intimidating than addressing why I'm so unlovable."

"What do you mean you're not lovable?" There was a sharp intake of breath, almost like my words had caused Sarah physical pain. "That's why you've been so gung ho about Mars? I can't believe I missed it all this time. Lizzie, look me in the eyes."

I didn't want to because my eyes were waterlogged, and when I blinked, the tears overflowed.

"You are very lovable," she said, those little muscles in her jaw flexing with each word. "Don't ever think for one second you aren't."

"Then why didn't my parents think so? The two people on this planet who should have loved me, didn't. That does more damage than I truly understood until these past few months. Before I figured out why I'm so annoying."

"You're not annoying." There went that clenching again.

"You seem pretty annoyed right now," I pointed out.

Frankly, even I wanted to smack myself for wallowing in a sea of self-pity.

"I'm not annoyed, honey. I'm sad. I hate that you think this way about yourself." Sarah walked around the island to pull me into her arms.

"Why can't I move to Mars?" I sobbed against her shoulder, shaking from head to toe. "I want to start over, get it right this time."

"You don't have to start over because there's nothing wrong with you. Not one thing." She squeezed me so hard I could picture my body cracking into two, but I couldn't bear the thought of her letting go.

When I was finally able to get control of myself enough to pull away and stand upright without wobbling, I checked the time on the microwave. "He'll be here in thirteen minutes. I don't know if I can do this."

"You can, and I think you should have a heart-to-heart with him."

"It's too late, Sarah. He made his choice when he checked out of my life and started a new family with Helen."

"It's never too late when it comes to a child."

"I'm almost forty with four kids. I'm not his child anymore. I'm a grown-up." *With some serious baggage,* I could easily have added. Not like she, of all people, didn't already know.

"Yes, you are a grown woman. You're also still his daughter. You have to talk to him, or these thoughts will always haunt you."

"I don't think I can," I whispered. "I only know how to confront you, and that's because you press my buttons until I explode. Now I'm crying. I blame you. Can't I check into a hotel and read about Mars? That'll make me happy."

"I'm sorry. I wish I had known all this before I spoke to your father."

"Would you still have green-lit his trip?"

"Yes."

I tried laughing, but it only made the tears come harder, so I snuggled my head into the crook of her neck, needing to feel safe.

"He's coming to see you, so you do matter. If you want him to play a bigger role in your life—and I suspect you do, or you wouldn't be this upset—you have to talk to him." Sarah ran a hand up and down my back.

"It scares me."

"I understand, but I also know when you face something you don't want to, you come out on top. For so many years, you fought the world all alone. You don't have to do that anymore. Open up. Let others take some of the burden onto their shoulders."

If only I knew how.

CHAPTER TWENTY-FIVE

"Gramps!" Ollie ran toward my father as soon as he walked through the door.

"Oh, how I missed you, Ollie Dollie." He got down on one knee to hug her, pulling her in so tightly I felt something akin to jealousy. Had he ever done that with me?

His heartfelt tone tugged me in twenty different directions. I may not have known my own feelings, but I knew I couldn't cut him out of my life because it'd hurt my own children, who loved their grandfather. Somehow, I needed to make peace with him, and if Sarah was right, I had to have a heart-to-heart with the man.

Fred and Demi had joined the hug-a-thon. Sarah squeezed my hand, giving me a supportive look and whispering, "It's going to be okay."

"Where's Calvin?" My father slowly got back on both feet, his knees and lower back creaking and popping.

"He's sleeping," I answered, "but he should be waking—"

Calvin's cry filled the house.

"That's my cue!" Before anyone could say otherwise, I dashed upstairs to tend to my youngest and quite possibly to forestall the inevitable. The truth was, while Sarah had all the confidence in me that I could talk to my father like a mature woman who'd grown a lot over the years, I'd rather hide under the bed and come out when Dad and Helen left.

Cal wiggled on the changing table to speed up the process, which, in fact, did the opposite. It was like he knew his siblings had gotten their hugs, and he wanted his.

"Okay, buddy, I'm hurrying." I snapped his pants back into place. "Aren't you a handsome fella!" I smoothed his hair, wild from sleep and the humidity. I hadn't checked a mirror. Mine probably was the same. "Maybe I should get a hairbrush, huh?"

"No!" He gave me side eye followed by an exasperated grunt as if saying, "I know what you're doing. Let's go!"

Thwarted in my attempts to stall any longer, I carried him on my hip down the stairs.

"He's gotten so big." Helen put her hands out to take Calvin.

"He'll be three this fall," I said. Sticking with facts wasn't so bad. I could do facts.

"I can't believe it. I'm commanding you not to grow another inch, young man. You're the baby in the family." Helen tickled Calvin's belly, causing him to coo. "I see he's getting over his grumpy stage."

Calvin's brow instantly furrowed. "No!"

"That's his favorite word, and he picks and chooses his grumpy moments." I laughed. His age stuck in my head, and I pondered aloud, "I doubt he'll go to preschool this fall. The twins have missed an entire year. They're supposed to start kindergarten, but I'm not sure that's wise. We've been going back and forth on it."

"By that, Lizzie means she's been arguing with me until she's blue in the face." Sarah jabbed a playful elbow into my side. "Come September, they'll be starting school."

"I don't feel comfortable sending them to school during a pandemic."

"Things are getting better," Sarah said in a singsong way.

"Less than half of the population is vaccinated!" I argued, preparing to dig in my heels for a good, long debate.

Sarah put a stop to that before I'd even gotten started. "The numbers in Massachusetts are better than most. This isn't the time to rehash whether or not we send the twins to school this fall. They're going."

"I'm with Lizzie," my father said. "It's too early, but I won't say another word."

I was about to tell him he was wrong when I realized he'd taken my side. What the hell? I hadn't expected that.

"I worry that they're not getting socialized." Sarah stopped herself after getting one final word in, which was one of her specialties. "You two must be exhausted from your trip."

"Not at all." My father's eyes shimmered with excitement. "It's been ages since I drove a car, and now I've racked up the miles."

"Leaving a trail of destruction in his path." Helen patted his cheek.

"You're the one who took out a curb."

"A love tap doesn't equate to taking out a curb," Helen said, waving a hand as if to dismiss the very thought of whatever had transpired.

Try as I might, I couldn't recall a conversation like this between my father and mother. Could I blame the man for wanting someone like Helen in his life? Who was I to begrudge another human for wanting love? It was what I craved, and what I'd found with Sarah.

Damn. The whipsawing of my thoughts and emotions was exhausting.

"How are—?" Helen began.

"Tea! Would anyone like tea?" I clapped my hands together,

nipping Helen's simple question in the bud. Questions required answers, and I was fresh out.

"Yes, please," Sarah said, knowing I needed to escape for a bit to regroup my thoughts. Little did she know I wanted the time to devise a way to tunnel out of the basement. Not being the gardening type, I wasn't sure we even owned a shovel. What other implement could I use?

In the kitchen, while I was filling up the electric kettle, Maddie and Willow came through the garage door, both looking as if they'd found out they had only weeks to live.

"Everything okay?" I plopped tea bags into different mugs.

"We can't buy a house." Maddie slumped down on one of the barstools.

"I'm going to get changed and go for a run." With that, Willow left, on the verge of tears.

"What happened with the mortgage lady? Everyone in the neighborhood recommended her, according to Sarah's Facebook posse." I grabbed another mug for Maddie.

"While my income is good now, it hasn't been for years, and with Willow technically being unemployed, we're too much of a risk."

"She's doing the podcast, and we have a sponsor. Our listening numbers are going up each week." I didn't give voice to the fact the money coming in was peanuts, but it was showing promise to grow into something much bigger with enough TLC and luck.

"The podcast venture is in its infancy." Maddie cradled her forehead with a palm. "I think Willow thought it would be easier. She's the positive type, and she found out we have a tough hill to climb."

This was proof as to why it paid off to always believe nothing would work out, but I didn't think that was the type of sentiment Maddie needed from me at this exact point in time. I filed it away for the future. "What can be done in the meantime?"

"Rent a place, I guess."

"Prices are sky-high right now for rent, same as for houses. Won't that cut into your savings for the down payment?"

Maddie simply nodded, seeming too exhausted to put much thought into anything.

I remembered Sarah telling me recently not to focus on saving all of humanity, but to look to smaller things, like helping my family where I could. Maddie and Willow fell into that category, so I wanted to do something to help, which was why I blurted out, "Our basement isn't finished."

Maddie gave me an odd look.

"Uh, I probably should talk to Sarah first, but what if we finish the basement? There's a door, so you two would have a private entrance. I know it's not a house, per se, but you can stay here until you can buy a place of your own." I whirled around to look out the kitchen window. "I've been doing some research into a she-shed for Sarah. She never gets a break from the kids, or me for that matter, and I would like to create a space she can disappear to. Otherwise, I think she might lop off my head. Can you help me get quotes for the basement and she-shed and find people you trust for the construction? We'll also need to move the podcast equipment out of the basement into your old room, when the basement is habitable. I can't imagine that would require much work." What other details was I missing? Probably a million.

"You'd really do that for us?"

"Like I said, I need to run it by Sarah." I briefly put up a hand, letting it fall back to my side. "But I can't imagine she'd say no. She loves having everyone around her like a mother hen. I'm the one who's always disappearing for Lizzie time. Like now, I guess."

"Who are you hiding from now?" Maddie glanced about the kitchen.

"What's taking you so—oh, hi Maddie. What's wrong?" Sarah rubbed Maddie's back, looking to me for an answer, or perhaps laying the blame at my feet.

"The mortgage meeting didn't go well," I offered. "I'm almost done with the tea, but in the meantime, what do you think about finishing the basement so Maddie and Willow can have a space of their own while they figure out their housing situation? Where's the honey?" My eyes bounced around all the counter space. "It's usually by the toaster, but I don't see it."

Sarah reached into the pantry, retrieving a new jar. "One problem solved, and what's this about the basement?"

I froze, not reaching for the jar she held out to me.

Maddie took it out of Sarah's hand, scooting it over the island to me. "It was only an idea. Nothing concrete, and Lizzie did say she should run it by you." Maddie looked to me and then back at Sarah, like maybe she wasn't too thrilled at getting caught in the middle.

"I probably should have done that before mentioning it to Maddie." I hitched my shoulders, offering up my *please don't kill me* expression.

Sarah shook her head, laughing. "I think it's a wonderful idea."

"You're not mad?"

"Surprised is more like it. For someone who continually claims she doesn't like being around people, you bend over backward to make everyone happy."

The kettle flipped off, and I poured hot water into all of the mugs.

Sarah started counting them. "We need one more for Troy."

"He's here already? I promised one to Maddie, so I need two

more, I think." I shook the kettle. "I have to boil another pot. You guys go ahead. I got this."

"Okay, but you can only hide for so long, dear." Sarah carried the tray into the front room.

Maddie came around the island, giving me a kiss on the cheek.

"What was that for? Saving your tea?" I rubbed my skin, having to resist the urge to wipe the wetness from my hand, hoping she'd turn her head soon so I could do exactly that.

"For being you. I'm going to tell Willow the news before she leaves, and then I'll do my best to run interference for you during this visit."

"Before you go, please don't mention the she-shed to Sarah. I want it to be a surprise. I was thinking of it being her Christmas gift, but that's still five months away." I started to second-guess my idea on so many levels. "Or will she be mad about being left out since she loves crafting to-do lists?"

"What about this? I can tell her I'm working on one for a client who doesn't know what she wants besides a she-shed and get Sarah's input as part of the ruse. That way she'll be creating her own but won't know."

"That's brilliant!" I practically jumped in the air. "Now, go put Willow out of her misery, hopefully, and then…" I mouthed the words *my father*.

CHAPTER TWENTY-SIX

"Wow, it's been so long since we've had a family dinner including Lizzie's parents." Sarah set the salad bowl in the middle of the table and took her seat across from me.

I was about to dispute the parents part strictly based on the definition of the word, but then I realized Helen had been more of a mom to me these past few years than my own ever had, so I reinforced the thought with, "It really has."

My father's eyes became teary, but he didn't say anything, squeezing his wife's hand instead.

"I can't believe you drove all the way here." Maddie finished pouring wine into everyone's glasses, setting the bottle off to the side on the hutch.

"I'm not sure when I'll be comfortable flying again." My father's voice sounded deeper than normal, or maybe I wasn't used to hearing it in person after such a long separation. Either way, it was stirring up emotions that were making my belly clench.

"I second that," I said, doing all I could to keep the conversation on safe ground. "I still remember frantically trying to get back to Massachusetts, and Sarah screaming at me on the phone the entire time."

"I don't scream." She flashed a loving smile.

I beamed a naughty smile in her direction. "Oh, you do." I stuck a finger in my ear, shaking it about and wincing a bit. "I can still hear it."

She playfully gnashed her teeth at me. Meanwhile, I continued to prod my ear with my fingertip, finding it tender to the touch. When had that started?

"What's been new with you, Lizzie?" my father asked, scooping salad onto his plate while I sat frozen in my chair.

Dear God, was he going to open up the A-word chat during dinner?

"Not too much." My brain kicked into hyperdrive with ways to get him off the topic. "Did you know xing isn't a word? I only recently found that out. Xing with an X, not a Z. Is zing with a Z a word? I guess it is because zinger is." I took a breath but wasn't able to keep from saying, "Ollie has taken to shouting zing and then punching me in the arm, so you're forewarned."

All eyes were on me, and Sarah failed miserably at not laughing, which was a relief because if she hadn't, I'd worry she thought I was too far gone and needed to be institutionalized.

My father was about to speak, but I butted in again with, "I also learned all dairy cows are girls. I don't mean I thought boys produce milk. I mean in the pastures of dairy farms, they're all girls because the boys cause problems. Although, the girls pee and poop constantly, so there's that. I wonder if the boys piss and shit more than the girls."

Maddie, Willow, and Sarah gawked at me.

Rose, Troy, Helen, and my father all looked in different directions, none of them in mine.

I wanted to take my knife and stab it as hard as possible into my heart to see if maybe that would put a stop to my babbling. All of a sudden, I was having to remind myself not to mention Sarah's former fear that Troy was a pedo because that conversation back in March hadn't gone over well at all. But I was struggling to keep the conversation going, if you could call what I was doing conversation. I think it'd be more accurately described as Exhibit A as to why I should be locked up and not allowed to speak to any humans, including my own family, because I was failing miserably. And I really felt compelled to mention the pedo thing. Oh, God.

Sarah took control, saving me from sure destruction. "Charles, how is Peter doing?"

"He's allowed to leave the house now and has been helping Gabe run the shops."

This news blew my mind. My brother had worked for my father, and Peter's financial entanglements were the cause of my father's early retirement because the board wanted to cut the Peter rip cord, which meant forcing my father out. Now, Peter was back in the fold, helping run Helen's flower business. Why did he always get another chance?

I stabbed at my salad, one of my concessions to eating more veggies to avoid a Sarah lecture, never quite managing to get more than one leaf of lettuce at a time. The conversation pinged around the table as I continued not to engage. I knew whatever I might say would go wrong in a hundred ways.

When it came time for dessert, I got to my feet, making a mad dash for the kitchen, and Maddie joined me.

"I thought you were going to play interference for me," I whispered.

"He hasn't said a thing about you being... ya know." She removed the glass cake lid, set it to the side, and used a knife to slice off eight pieces.

"Not that. Earlier when I was babbling about xings and dairy cows only being girls, why didn't you throw me a rope?"

"I was too afraid you'd hang yourself with it," she spoke with heartfelt honesty.

"You know, I used to complain all the time when you picked on me, but when I really needed you to intervene somehow, making me the butt of the joke or whatever you used to do to hijack a conversation, you left me out to dry. Rose, too. I wanted her to make car sounds like she used to, her way of saying she planned to run me over with her Cadillac. At least that way, my father would take pity on me. Well, he still might, but for different reasons, and he's possibly factoring how much it'd cost to lock me away. You and Rose let me down. Is it because everyone thinks I'm too fragile, given my A-status?"

"I can't speak for Rose, but Willow has been giving me shit about teasing you. And, yes, since learning about your auti—"

I covered her mouth with my hand.

Maddie scouted over her shoulder, making it hard for me to keep my hand in place, but I did. "What?" she forced out.

"We do not say the word. Not ever."

"Okay but you know you proclaimed it on your podcast."

"Not on purpose," I whisper-yelled. "That just came out of me. We don't intentionally talk about it."

"Unlike xings, and dairy cows being girls." She stepped back so I couldn't whack her. "Totally normal conversation for a grown woman."

"Don't waste that shit in here. Save me out there when I start rambling!" I pointed the cake knife she'd set down on the counter toward the dining room.

"I don't think anything can save you when you get on those kicks." Maddie shrugged. "Perhaps you should think happy thoughts and not speak much."

"That's what I've been doing. How do I distract when asked direct questions?" I took my notepad out of my shorts pocket to jot down whatever hints she could share.

Instead of giving me a list, Maddie covered my hand with hers. "Be yourself, Lizzie."

"My history proves that doesn't work in my favor."

"Poppycock."

"Since when do you say that word?"

Maddie looked deep into my eyes. "Stop worrying. Everything's going to be fine."

That was easy for everyone else to say. They didn't have to deal with the thoughts running through my head, but I couldn't exactly tell them what they were, or I'd definitely end up in an institution. I was coming completely unhinged.

CHAPTER TWENTY-SEVEN

Sarah sat on the side of the bed, staring down at me. "Do you intend to get up today?"

"I did, hours ago," I argued, even though I could see her point, given that I was in bed and all. "I'm napping now. It's a completely different thing."

"You're reading in bed at four in the afternoon."

"The kids are at your mom's," I grumped. "Why can't I relax?"

"Because," Sarah said in that soft tone that concealed a warning, "your father and stepmother are downstairs, and they drove all the way across the country to spend time with you."

"They only drove two-thirds of the way since they started in Colorado," I felt compelled to point out.

Sarah mimed she wanted to strangle me. Who could blame her, really? I was in a shitty mood and unfit for human company, which was why she should've been leaving me alone. This was totally her fault.

"I'm tired!" I pouted.

"You're hiding!" she countered.

"What if I am? Can't I hide in my own home?"

"Not with me around," she said, and no truer words had ever been spoken. She was as relentless as a bulldozer. Or a jackhammer. Or a machine that does both. Do they have those? "Lizzie, get out of bed, go downstairs, and talk to your father."

"I can't," I said flatly.

"Why not?" Yeah, definitely a bulldozing jackhammer.

"It won't go well," I snapped. "I'm really pissed, and besides, he's busy helping Peter get back on his feet."

Still not letting this go, Sarah said, "He came all this way to spend time with you. He wants to be there for you, not just Peter."

"I don't care. It makes me mad. I've been competing with Peter for so long, and I really thought, what with him being a convicted felon and all, I had a better shot, but no. Peter is working for Helen. They've never offered *me* a job."

"Probably because you have a steady career," Sarah pointed out with the air of someone who was determined to be practical in the face of a total hissy fit. "Also, you didn't recently get out of prison."

"You're missing the point. I'm so angry with everyone in my family, but I can't yell at my mom because she's dead. Unless you know someone with a connection to the afterlife. I may have finally worked up the nerve to tell her what I really think. I wimped out when I confronted her when she was dying. Yeah, I said some things, but I didn't completely unload on her. That bothers me to this day, but what was I supposed to do? She was dying. I couldn't dump all of my shit onto a dying woman, could I?" I took a deep breath, and only at that point did I notice how shaky it was, like I was gasping for oxygen.

Sarah uncurled my fingers, which were digging into one of her paperbacks because I didn't have any of my own books to read, or even my Kindle or phone, both of which I'd forgotten in the library when I absconded upstairs to nap. To state the obvious, yes, I was too chickenshit to venture downstairs in case my father cornered me to chat about the A-Word.

"Honey, I don't want you to live with that regret."

"Do you mean you know someone who can communicate with spirits?" I perked up in bed. "Can this person tell my mother to go to hell?"

"Uh, no." Sarah pursed her lips. "I was speaking about your father."

"I can't tell him to go to hell. He's still alive."

"Yes, which makes it a better time to talk to him."

"To his face?" I shrank back down in bed.

"I don't think this is a text or email situation," Sarah said. This was one of those rare times when she was unequivocally wrong. Obviously.

I smacked my hand down on the comforter. "I can't tell my father I'm upset that he was a shitty father."

"I know you hate conflict, and I understand." Sarah rested a hand on my shoulder, and half of me wanted to shake it off while the other half wanted to grasp it and hold on for dear life. "If it were me and one of our kids felt like you do, I'd want to know."

I swallowed, terrified. "Am I a shitty parent like my father?"

"No, honey, but if one of the kids was upset with you, wouldn't you want them to tell you?"

I wasn't sure of my answer. "On one hand, absolutely. On the other, ignorance is bliss."

"For whom?"

"I hate when you do that." I glared at her.

"Use proper English?" Lifting her hand from my shoulder, she ruffled my hair. "Or do you hate it when I'm right?"

"Yes."

Sarah's smile was wide. "I know."

"I don't know if I can do it, Sarah. The thought of it shuts down my brain." I circled a finger around my temple.

A WOMAN UNHINGED

Sarah grasped my hand and lifted it to her lips. "He loves you, Lizzie. I think you've learned to love him, too. Trust him to listen."

"What if he yells at me?" My voice sounded meek, like I was five. I'd probably be the one sent to kindergarten in the fall, not the twins. "I hate being yelled at."

Sarah's jaw flexed. "Then I'll punch him in the nose."

"You're going to be there?" This buoyed me some. I can't lie. I liked the mental image of her punching my father right in the honker.

"That was a joke, and no, I won't. This is a private conversation for the two of you, and it's long overdue."

CHAPTER TWENTY-EIGHT

SOMEHOW, we made it through three days of my father's visit without the dreaded A-word rearing its head, not even a glimpse or shadow of it. Part of me knew the clock was ticking and would eventually run out, but I also had hope. As yet another new day dawned, and I wasn't assaulted with questions about autism over my morning tea, I started to think that maybe I would be spared.

Much to my relief, Sarah had arranged a day trip to the ocean with Dad and Helen. Our car was packed with the kids, so my father and Helen followed us in their car. I mean, it wasn't like my father would call my phone while we were driving and we had all of the kids. I could keep one child next to me, meaning, my streak would continue throughout the day.

Perhaps Sarah had sniffed out my master plan because as soon as we reached the beach and unloaded the car, she immediately cornered Helen. "Why don't we take the kids to that playground over there? It'll give Lizzie and Charles time to talk."

My heart practically stopped beating, and my jaw nearly fell off its hinge.

"Excellent idea," Helen said, definitely in cahoots with my wife's evil plan.

"Come on, kids." Sarah clapped her hands in a very mom-like way. Even Ollie behaved, although I didn't think she was in on the whole *throwing me under the bus* thing. She wanted to play. Before I could register an objection, or possibly take one of the children hostage so I wouldn't be left alone to my fate, the whole family was halfway to the playground.

There we stood, my father and I, staring at the ocean, not speaking.

I started crafting a mental list of all the ways I could get back at Sarah. When I reached number twenty-one, Dad cleared his throat once but didn't say anything, so I kept my eyes trained on the water, adding three more items to my list.

The silence was killing me.

"It just goes on, doesn't it?" I was talking about the water, not the interminable silence between us or my list of ways to wreck Sarah's life for that matter, although it was amazing how many ideas I had brainstormed already. Sadly, I couldn't write them in my notebook because I feared my father would ask what I was jotting down so furiously.

"I don't know if I could live with a view of the ocean," my father said. "It's intimidating."

"Really?" This surprised me. My father was a larger-than-life figure in my mind. To imagine him being intimidated, let alone have him admit to it, was hard to comprehend. "I think I might like it. I can see myself sitting on a deck, with a book in hand, watching the ocean and listening to the waves crash onto the beach. It soothes me, knowing the tides keep coming and going no matter what."

"I think that's the part that disturbs me." He motioned to a nearby bench. "Sit?"

No, I didn't want to sit. I wanted to run until I couldn't run anymore. I still ended up saying, "Sure."

He moved slowly before taking his spot. Perhaps it was his recent admission about the ocean, but I couldn't help thinking he looked frailer than I remembered. His hair, which in my mind was as thick and dark as it had been in my childhood, had become sparse and white. His legs, already a shock to me to see bare in shorts instead of his usual office attire, were skinny and pale, and I could see the veins through the skin like a purple roadmap.

I sat next to him, considering all the possible subjects he might want to discuss. Sure, the A-word was the obvious choice. It was probably at the top of his list, but what if he was a Mars enthusiast as well, and I didn't know? That would be a pleasant turn of events. I was tempted to ask, but I knew I would start to babble, making things much worse.

I fiddled with a string on the hem of my T-shirt, not knowing where to start. He hadn't been the best father for the majority of my life, but we'd grown somewhat closer since I'd become a parent. As Sarah had said, I should let him in more, but that thought clogged my throat with fear, and I wasn't able to get words out. Not to mention, my heart still hadn't fully recovered from the whole stopping thing when Sarah gave voice to her sabotage.

Did he feel the same way? At his age, stopping his heart was more than a figure of speech. Wouldn't this type of stress risk his life? That was a strong argument in favor of not talking about anything ever again. I could live with that.

Or perhaps something else was going on. Maybe this desire to chat had nothing to do with me at all. Was he already dying? That was when my mother had started opening up to me, when she was scared of death. Maybe he'd been to the doctor recently, but instead of being told to drink more water, he'd been given six months to live.

Was that why he drove all this way? I couldn't think of any other reason for something so out of the ordinary. My father, who always had a driver, got into his car and traveled hundreds and hundreds of miles to see me. Why? It had to be because he was dying.

My body clenched, and my pulse quickened as I contemplated the terrible likelihood that I would soon be orphaned.

No. I couldn't accept it. This was Charles Allen Petrie we were talking about. The man was a legend in the finance world. My trust fund was proof of that. There was no way he'd let something as mundane and ordinary as death slow him down. Then again, after Peter's legal problems, Dad had been forced to quit work. Perhaps when he'd walked away from the empire he'd built, the spark inside him had gone out.

I turned to face him, slowly and cautiously. The plan was to try my best to uncover signs of impending doom without letting on that I knew, but when I looked into his eyes, I was absolutely floored to see tears. Instantly, I broke, panic hitting with the force of a wave against a rock.

"Oh God, you're really dying, aren't you?"

He pulled back, his eyes darting around like he was expecting to see a physical menace, perhaps a man wielding an axe or a wild grizzly bear charging toward him.

When no such threat materialized, he said, "No. Not that I'm aware of."

"That's a relief." It was. Much greater than I would have thought it would be three minutes prior to this point.

"I don't know how to say this," my father began, his voice shaky and uncertain, "but I want you to know how sorry I am for everything."

That was nice to hear but also extremely vague. There were a lot of things he might've been sorry about, like the year I didn't get a Smurfs drum set for Christmas, and I didn't want to assume that was the reason he'd spoken, so I asked, "What for?"

"After hearing on your podcast that you might be autistic, I started doing some digging, and…" He looked back at the ocean.

I swallowed hard, aware that we'd arrived at the moment I'd been dreading. The A-word was out there in the open, and there was no avoiding it any longer.

"There's, uh…" My hands were starting to shake, and I had to clench them into fists to keep them under control as adrenaline surged through every vein. "There's a lot of evidence pointing to yes."

He nodded solemnly. "That there is."

"I'm sorry," I whispered, shuffling my feet.

He shifted on the bench, looking me in the eyes again. He seemed baffled by what I'd said. "What are you sorry for?"

"I know it's got to be hard for a man like you to have a daughter like me." I'd never felt like such a complete failure in my life.

"What do you mean?"

"All of your peers always looked up to you. Then Peter got arrested, and things started to shift for you. Now, people are learning I'm autistic because I couldn't keep my mouth shut on my podcast. I shouldn't have made it harder for you."

"Don't you ever think that," he said firmly but not like he was scolding. "You have nothing to be sorry for. There's nothing wrong with you."

"I'm different."

"That you are." He chuckled softly, not at all angry or mortified as I'd expected. "It's one of the things I've always admired about you."

I shook my head, not really able to process what he was saying because it was so far from what I'd expected to hear. Maybe he wasn't getting it, and that's why he wasn't mad. "I keep thinking what Mom would say. The words she'd call me. *Retard* for one."

He sucked in a deep breath. "I don't like that word."

"It's an ugly one." I shuffled my feet in the dirt again, wishing I could lunge off this bench and run, swim, or any other method of escaping my reality. Why hadn't I ever mastered walking on my hands? "She was particularly fond of going for the jugular."

There was another deep breath, all the acknowledgement needed. We both knew what she'd been like.

"If you had known back then about me…" I shifted uncomfortably before starting again. "That is, if someone had said then that I was autistic, and if we'd known what that even was back then, would you have done anything differently?"

"Yes." His answer was immediate and emphatic. "Staying for so long with your mom is one of my big regrets."

"You told me a few years ago she threatened you. That she would destroy you, Helen, and your business if you left."

"She did, and it scared me. But you were miserable. I should have done something. More. I'm sorry." White head bowed, shoulders sagging, he looked like a man defeated. There might have been times when I thought I would want to see him brought low like this, but now that it was happening, it shattered my heart into a million shards, each poking my chest, actually causing pain. Even so, I couldn't stop speaking now that the floodgates had been opened.

"For many years," I said, my eyes fixed on the sea, "I thought you didn't have the parenting gene. Then I met Allen, and while I'm not saying it's his fault in any way, I've wondered a lot lately why Allen deserved a happy family with my father, and I didn't matter."

"Lizzie," he began, but I shook my head.

"No, I need to say this. It's been difficult to live with." I let out a sigh. "The thing is for so many years, I didn't have anyone looking out for me. Mom hated me. Peter tormented me to win points with Mom. You worked all the time. I was entirely alone. Well, there was Annie, but she was paid to watch me, and even as a kid, I understood the difference between a nanny and a parent. Not that she was unkind. She was quite kind. But it was hard to believe she really liked me when you guys didn't, and I convinced myself she was only pretending because you paid her well to treat me that way."

Again, I shuffled my feet in the dirt, wondering if I should keep going or if that was enough. Meanwhile, my father didn't say a word. So, I pressed on.

"It wasn't until I met Sarah that I learned someone could love me even if I am different. I kept most people at arm's length before her, not wanting to risk being rejected again because even my own parents and brother did for as long as I could remember. Meg was terrible to me, and I let her be. I didn't think I mattered much or that I could expect to be treated well, or even halfway decently." I steadied my breathing as much as possible to continue. "Sarah. She was the first to love me. Now, I have four amazing kids. I never get alone time anymore, but it's okay. There were many days before Sarah when I really didn't see the point to anything. I think it's why I studied so much. To keep my brain from planting dangerous thoughts into my head."

"Such as?" He said it quietly, and I thought perhaps the prospect of my answer intimidated him as much as the Atlantic Ocean.

"I'd rather not say, but they were unpleasant. Sometimes, I'm shocked I'm still here. That I've made it to almost forty." I paused, not wanting to continue but feeling I needed to. "For so long, I didn't want to be. It was kind of a comforting thought, knowing I could stop being. Even if I had nothing else, I could control that part of my life. Now, I'm trying to learn everything I can to save humanity. It's such an odd thought for me. I blame Sarah." This time when I laughed, I meant it. "Being a parent to four kids who I want to give the world to is exhausting. I keep trying to figure out all the contingency plans to ensure they'll never suffer, even when I can't be here for them anymore, which I hope is decades and decades from now. I have my sights on living to at least a hundred. Another irony, considering ten years ago, I lived by my five-year plans."

Shit.

As soon as I realized what I'd said, I shut my mouth, instantly falling silent. What had I been thinking? I didn't talk about that with anyone. It was even more a forbidden topic than autism. Maybe I wasn't as good at navigating forbidden topics as I thought I was.

My father, meanwhile, was studying me intensely. He didn't say anything, but there was a question in his eyes, along with a wild, desperate look that told me he knew what I was talking about but didn't want to be right.

"Yeah, so every time I made it another five years, I'd weigh the pros and cons of sticking around. It was a ritual, I guess. Once I decided, I had to go another five years. That was the rule." I glanced over my shoulder at my family, a sense of peace coming over me as I watched the little ones at play. "I wouldn't change it, though. They're great kids."

"When—" His voice sounded strangled, like his larynx was being crushed by an anvil. He cleared his throat and tried again. "When did you start contemplating your five-year plans?"

"Oh gosh, I'm not sure." I blew out a breath as I tried to recall, aiming it so the air hit my forehead and would have moved the hair if it weren't already being tossed to and fro in the sea breeze. "I was ten, maybe, the first time. I think I built up that birthday in my head because I'd be in the double digits. Somehow it was a magical number, and I'd finally be accepted into the family fold. Then the special day came and went. I didn't get a cake or a gift. Not even a pack of gum as an afterthought. It kinda hit me at that moment. It wasn't my age that was the problem. It was me."

There was a sharp intake of breath, but I didn't turn my head. I didn't want to see the look on his face.

"Can you do me a favor?" I asked, staring at the horizon, the water going on and on.

"Yes," he replied, his tone gravelly and rough.

"Don't tell anyone about my five-year plans." I rocked slightly, thinking about what others would say if they knew. "I've never talked about it. Not even in therapy. I'm not sure why I told you."

Out of the corner of my eye, I saw him nod, but he didn't say a word.

We continued to sit, side by side, looking at the ocean.

CHAPTER TWENTY-NINE

"Shall we seek out the others?" I asked after several quiet moments, not knowing what else to say or do. My father and I were seated exactly as we had been for who knows how long, and my bottom was starting to go numb.

"Go ahead," he said softly, his words devoid of any emotion. "I'll be there soon."

"Okay." A trickle of fear made its way through my skull as I contemplated my father, completely shut down beside me. Perhaps, Sarah had been wrong. He didn't want to know my thoughts. I'd crossed so far over the line that I'd rendered him speechless.

I trudged across the grassy area beyond the sand until I finally found everyone outside an ice cream place next to the playground. Naturally. Come hell or high water, there's always ice cream.

Sarah perked up in her seat as soon as she saw me, a look of eager anticipation in her eyes. "How'd it go?"

I shrugged, struggling to get my shaky legs under the picnic table.

"You two talked, didn't you?" She regarded me suspiciously,

as if she could picture us both sitting there for however long it had been, not saying a word. That probably would've been better, in retrospect.

"Yes," I said, pinching my eyes closed to avoid replaying it in my mind. It didn't work as well as I'd hoped. "Well, I did most of the talking. I'm not sure if he heard me, though."

Helen set her ice cream cup down. "Did he ask you questions?"

"A few maybe." It was all kind of a blur now. Did I really tell him about my five-year plans? I hadn't thought of those in so long. Why did I tell him? The A-word was one thing, but that? That was on a whole different level of shit one never gave voice to.

"Did he do anything else?" Helen pressed.

"He stared at the water. Laser-locked on it really." I didn't mention that at one point I wanted to put a mirror in front of his face to see if he was still breathing. I mean, it wasn't like I'd done it, so I hardly needed to confess. I'd done enough of that for one day.

"Then, he was listening to every single word you said," Helen announced with confidence. "Now, he's processing. Soon, he'll come up with a plan."

"For what?" I bunched my eyebrows. I'd had about enough of plans of any sort, five-year or otherwise.

"To fix things," she said simply.

"But we talked about my childhood. It's not like he can build a time machine and fix it," I argued. Then I stopped, getting a vision of what that would be like. "If he did build a time machine, that would be awesome. I'd love to get firsthand experience about some time periods."

Helen gave me a kind smile. "He may not be able to fix things in the past, but he's always looking for ways to make things right in the present. Even more so now."

I was about to ask what she meant by that, but Helen stood and said, "I'll go check on him."

When she was gone, I whispered to Sarah, "If he's dying, I'm going to feel like a huge schmuck for laying all of what I said at his feet. He said he wasn't, but was he lying?" I ran a hand over my head. "This is your fault."

Sarah arched an eyebrow. "How?"

"You told me not to hold back, so I didn't. Now, I feel terrible. Absolutely terrible."

CHAPTER THIRTY

MY FATHER and Helen approached the table, walking hand in hand. As my heart raced, Sarah squeezed my leg under the picnic table. Whatever was going to happen, at least I knew I had her there. I wished I didn't feel so scared.

My father offered me a shy, half-smile, in the way he did when he had no idea what to say, but it was friendlier than in the days when I still lived under the same roof with him, the Scotch-lady, and Peter. It was a better start than I'd hoped for, to be honest. My pulse slowed.

"Should the kids and I go?" Sarah started to stand, but Dad waved for her to retake her seat.

"Please stay," he said. "This affects all of you."

What did that mean? Once again, I braced for the worst, which I assumed might be him declaring he never wanted to talk to me again. When I'd met Sarah, I wasn't in contact with my family, so it wasn't like being cut off was weird for me, but so much had happened over the past seven or eight years, and not having my father again would leave a gaping hole in my life. To be honest, it always had been there, but I would feel it even more now because the older I got, I found it was harder to shut off my emotions. Like the shutoff valve that allowed me to do it for years had refused to work anymore.

I dug my fingernails into the palm of my right hand to prevent tears from falling. It'd been a trick I'd developed when I was a kid, when mother was ridiculing me in front of an audience. Sometimes, I'd actually drawn blood.

Dad sat across from me, Helen settling next to him, offering me a *you're going to be all right* smile.

Still, I dug my nails deeper. Was that a drop of blood?

"I know that wasn't easy for you, Lizzie," my dad finally managed to say, not quite making eye contact but not sounding angry, which was promising. "I'm so very proud of you."

Had I heard him right? My eyes started to water, and I wasn't sure if they were happy, sad, or relieved tears.

He looked to Helen. "We've decided to move out here to be close to you."

"You're moving to Massachusetts?" My eyes had probably doubled in size at this announcement, and for good reason. Out of all of the possibilities I'd run through in my head, this hadn't been one of them.

"If that's okay with you two," Helen added gently, softening my dad's gruffness in the way she always did. "We don't want to be in the way."

I didn't know what to say, but when Sarah nudged my leg with hers, I knew I needed to respond.

"I don't understand. Your businesses," I said to Helen and then added, "and Peter. Who's going to look after him?"

"Gabe is the answer to both questions," Helen replied. "He's taking over the shops, and Peter will help out with the one in Denver. He's actually taken a shine to it."

I blinked.

Dad laughed. "It surprised me, too, because I never suspected Peter would love running a flower shop."

"It's been a kick watching him make flower arrangements. They're quite lovely," Helen said.

"Will he be okay?" A few days ago, when I learned Peter was helping with the shops, I had been upset, jealous my father was standing by my brother after everything. Now, I was worried about Peter, who hadn't made the wisest of decisions. Would he feel as abandoned as I once had? I was surprised to find I didn't want that for him. Not at all. Probably because I knew what it did to someone. Fucked them up beyond belief.

"He's been clear that he wants to stand on his own two feet. I admire that about him," my father said.

"I should be doing that as well," I responded, feeling ashamed at how badly I wanted my father and Helen to stay close by. I had no right to expect it, but I wanted it so much. I didn't want to stand on my own anymore. Did that make me bad or place me at the bottom of the Petrie totem pole all over again?

He sucked in a shaky breath. "Haven't you been doing that for too long, Lizzie?"

"I—" I broke down.

CHAPTER THIRTY-ONE

THE NEXT MORNING, I woke with a start and possibly a scream.

"What's wrong?" Sarah sprung up next to me, her fists out and ready to battle whatever malevolent force was in the room.

"You're still here." I fell back onto the bed, utterly exhausted.

She slanted her head, her brow furrowing. "It's early. Where'd you think I'd gone?"

"Away. With the kids." I shuddered over the fading memory of wandering the empty house, my voice echoing. "Even the furry ones."

She seemed to catch on rather quickly, a feat given it was barely light out. "Lizzie. I'm not leaving, and even if I did make a break for it, I'd leave the kids, along with Hank and Gandhi, with you. Being a single parent of our brood scares the shit out of me."

I laughed. "Thanks for keeping it real."

Concern flooded her eyes. "One of your dreams?"

I nodded, not wanting to discuss it now that my brain had

caught up with the fact that I was awake and nothing traumatic had actually happened. "I've been on edge, lately. That's all."

"I know, which is why I think I need to confess something."

I gaped at her.

"Nothing bad. Settle." She placed a hand over my heart. "Settle."

"I had started to calm down until you said you need to tell me something. Nothing good has ever come after someone uttered those words." I reiterated, "Nothing at all."

"Well, this might blow your mind, then, because what I have to confess is something good. Fantastic really." She bounced on the bed like a child.

I eyed her with suspicion.

"The real reason your father came was for a surprise birthday party. One that he wanted help planning."

"My father planned a surprise birthday party?" I wasn't believing the words arriving at my ears, and I went to shake a finger in one, wincing in pain.

"That's enough with the ear torture device, okay? You're going to end up deaf."

"I seem to be the only one experiencing pain, though. I need to toughen up."

Sarah's eyes fell to the bed comforter. "Um, that may be because we stopped using them very early on."

"How early?"

"A day or two, perhaps three."

I blinked.

"Before you go all environmental on me, I purchased some that are made of bamboo, the sustainably grown kind, organic cotton, and are BPA-free. It's the second-best option, according to my research. After the kind that is destroying your ears."

"It's not destroying them." I tucked one ear down to my shoulder in case she stuck a finger in it to hammer home her point, although Sarah was never the type who enjoyed inflicting pain.

"While I admire your newfound dedication to solving the world's climate crisis, I think you need to realize you are only one person. You, and we, as a family can do what we can to help, but you alone cannot save the planet. That doesn't mean I'm not on board with making necessary changes for our family. It's important you admit that's all we can do."

"Not having a planet will wreck everything for everyone."

"I'm aware, but again, I want to stress you are only one person. You are not responsible for everything under the sun."

"I want—hold on. Why are you guys planning a surprise birthday party for the twins? It's July. Not August."

She stared so deeply into my eyes I imagined her gaze slamming into the back of my skull, bouncing around like a pinball, because apparently, I was missing something so obvious that she'd been rendered speechless.

"What?" I asked, wishing she'd break her gaze.

"It's July fourteenth."

"Yes, not the twins' birthday." I thought I'd already established that fact.

"Correct. It's not their birthday. It's yours."

"Mine?" I hit my chest with my palm. "You planned a surprise birthday party for me—er, my father did?" Happiness flooded me until realization booted it to the side. "Did he do this after my five-year plan confession at the ocean?"

"It was before he arrived, and what plan are you talking about?"

Dammit!

"Nothing. We better get going. Do I get cake today? I live for cake." I tossed the covers off of me, starting to scramble out.

She yanked me back. "You always get cake on your birthday."

"Not when I was a kid."

"I'm really sorry about that, but it'll never happen again on my watch."

Once again, I kicked the covers off, reenergized knowing cake was on the horizon.

Sarah pulled the covers back over me. "You're not getting out of this bed until you tell me about the five-year plan."

"How about we do something else in bed?" I cuddled up next to her, kissing the side of her neck, which she covered with a palm.

"Now, Lizzie!"

"It was nothing. The simple whims of a child." I tried shrugging it off.

"Not buying that because after your chat, your father and Helen decided to move here. Something scared the bejeezus out of him, and I want to know what."

"I don't want to scare you, though." It was amazing that she hadn't tried to pry out what had really scared my father to decide within half an hour of my confession to uproot not only his but Helen's life.

She bore her dark eyes into mine, and I tried to stay strong, lasting roughly 3.4 seconds before wilting and telling her what I'd told my father.

When I finished, she said, "You were ten when you implemented this plan?"

I nodded. "The first one at least."

"Oh, Lizzie. No wonder you drive yourself crazy ensuring the kids are taken care of and know we love them."

"So, I can keep using the ear thing? Yes, they hurt, but the planet—"

"Absolutely not. No going deaf. I like it when you can hear me and the children."

"I'm sure your screeching, and the kids', could penetrate any wall of silence."

She shook her head, the sadness still evident in the crinkles around her eyes. "Not on my watch. Now, let's get the big day going because I never ever want you to think of those five-year plans ever again."

I HEARD the words before seeing the flickering candles on the cake in Sarah's hands as she led the group through the kitchen to the dining room, with the most bizarre version of "Happy Birthday" because all of the kids were on different words of the song.

Confused, I looked at my Fitbit, seeing it was only one minute after nine in the morning. I'd expected the surprise party to start in the evening, and I wasn't mentally prepared for it. Although, there was cake. That would blunt everything else.

Sarah placed the cake in front of me, right next to my discarded plate with the grapefruit rind. "Make a wish."

I tilted my head toward the ceiling, closed my eyes, and wished the cake had the magical ability to keep replenishing, because given the size of our family, we'd sadly only get one slice each. Then, I blew out the candles, much to the cheers, and with the help of Freddie, who had climbed into my lap.

"Happy birthday, darling." Sarah kissed my forehead.

Freddie swiveled his head, landing a sloppy kiss on my chin.

Rose started slicing pieces of cake, putting them on plates, which Helen passed around as everyone retook their seats.

"I've never had a breakfast birthday cake!"

Helen placed a massive piece in front of me, and Fred plunged his finger into the frosting and sucked on it.

"He takes after you and your love of cake." Sarah's eyes were glistening.

"I know it's early, but we've made some mimosas. A virgin one for you, Lizzie." My father set down the flute by my cake.

I glanced at Sarah, who'd gone to great lengths to ensure everything would please me, including not having bubbly in my glass.

After everyone had a drink, my father stayed on his feet, with his flute raised high. "To my beautiful daughter on her thirty-eighth. Wishing you sixty-two more wonderful years and then some."

I wasn't great at numbers, but I knew he'd done the math to reach one hundred, the year I told him I was aiming for. He had listened to every single word I'd spoken that day on the bench by the ocean.

Maddie scooted a tablet over to me, and I saw Peter with a glass of orange juice in a similar flute. "Happy birthday, Baby Sis."

"Hear, hear." Gabe came into view with his own glass.

"I can't believe you're all here." My eyes roved everyone in the room, including Troy and Willow, the newest members in the Petrie family.

"Always," my father and Peter said in unison, Peter adding, "Next year in the flesh."

My eyes teared up, but Ollie let out a screech, her face covered in frosting, making everyone laugh, all pairs of eyeballs in the room looking at her.

Aside from my father, who whispered, "I love you."

I'd lucked out in the family department. Not only did I wish the cake would never end, I didn't want the sun to set on this birthday.

A HUGE THANK YOU!

First, thanks so much for reading *A Woman Unhinged*. When I published *A Woman Lost*, which turned out to be my first book series, I had no idea the impact Lizzie would have on so many. I've received countless emails from readers who have confessed how much she means to them. It wasn't until I announced the end of the series that I realized how many love her. I have to admit while it's flattering, it's also intimidating because I fear I'll eventually mess up the Lizzie arc, letting down readers.

However, that's the risk a writer has to take with every single story they publish. And, I feel like I should say this right now. Lizzie's story will continue. Ideas are already percolating in my head, but I have to let them sit a bit before tackling the next installment.

I've published more than twenty-five novels, and I still find it simply amazing that people read my stories. When I hit publish on my first book back in 2013, after staring at the publish button for several days before I worked up the nerve to finally press it, I had no idea what would happen.

Years later, I still panic when I'm about to publish a new project, but it's because of your support that I find the courage

A HUGE THANK YOU!

to do it. My publishing career has been a wonderful journey, and I wouldn't be where I am today without you cheering me on.

If you enjoyed the story, I would really appreciate a review. Even short reviews help immensely.

Finally, don't forget if you want to stay in touch, sign up for my newsletter. I'll send you a free copy of *A Woman Lost* (just in case you don't have it yet), book 1 in the A Woman Lost series, plus the bonus chapters and *Tropical Heat* (a short story), all of which are exclusive to subscribers. And, you'll be able to enter monthly giveaways to win one of my books.

You'll also be one of the firsts to hear about many of my misadventures, like the time I accidentally ordered thirty pounds of oranges, instead of five. To be honest, that stuff happens to me a lot.

Here's the link to join: http://eepurl.com/hhBhXX

And, thanks again for letting Lizzie into your hearts.

ABOUT THE AUTHOR

TB Markinson is an American who's recently returned to the US after a seven-year stint in the UK and Ireland. When she isn't writing, she's traveling the world, watching sports on the telly, visiting pubs in New England, or reading. Not necessarily in that order.

Her novels have hit Amazon bestseller lists for lesbian fiction and lesbian romance. For a full listing of TB's novels, please visit her Amazon page.

Feel free to visit TB's website to say hello. On the *Lesbians Who Write* weekly podcast, she and Clare Lydon dish about the good, the bad, and the ugly of writing. TB also runs I Heart Lesfic, a place for authors and fans of lesfic to come together to celebrate and chat about lesbian fiction.

Want to learn more about TB. Hop over to her *About* page on her website for the juicy bits. Okay, it won't be all that titillating, but you'll find out more

Printed in Great Britain
by Amazon